SCOTT CONNOR

◆

CLEARWATER JUSTICE

Complete and Unabridged

LINFORD
Leicester

First published in Great Britain in 2005 by
Robert Hale Limited
London

First Linford Edition
published 2006
by arrangement with
Robert Hale Limited
London

British Library CIP Data

Connor, Scott
    Clearwater justice.—Large print ed.—
Linford western library
1. Western stories
2. Large type books
I. Title
823.9′2 [F]

ISBN 1–84617–508–9

Published by
F. A. Thorpe (Publishing)
Anstey, Leicestershire

Set by Words & Graphics Ltd.
Anstey, Leicestershire
Printed and bound in Great Britain by
T. J. International Ltd., Padstow, Cornwall

This book is printed on acid-free paper

CLEARWATER JUSTICE

For five years Deputy Jim Lawson had wanted to find his brother Benny's murderer. So when suspect Tyler Coleman rides into Clearwater, Jim slaps him in jail. But the outlaw Luther Wade arrives, threatening to break Tyler out of jail. Then Jim's investigation unexpectedly links Benny's murder to the disappearance of Zelma Hayden, the woman he had once hoped to marry. Can Jim uncover the truth before the many guns lining up against him deliver their own justice?

1

When Sheriff Cliff Hopeman showed two fingers, Deputy Jim Lawson faced the door. When Hopeman showed one finger, Jim slipped his Peacemaker from its holster.

And when Hopeman lowered that finger, Jim kicked open the door.

The door slammed back against the wall, but before it could rebound, Jim leapt into the hotel room with Hopeman at his heels.

Inside, two men stood by a table. A third man sat at the table. All were packing guns.

As Hopeman and Jim skidded to a halt both the standing men hurled their hands to their holsters, but Hopeman ripped lead into the man on the left's guts, spinning him to the floor. And Jim thundered a high slug into the man on the right's chest, which lifted his feet from the floor before he crashed into the wall.

A second slug ensured he was dead before he hit the floor.

Then Hopeman and Jim stood side by side, their guns trained on the sitting man.

'Reach,' Jim said, 'or die.'

The man at the table snorted.

'You can't go bursting in here making demands and shooting up — '

'I'm Deputy Lawson and this is Sheriff Hopeman.' Jim rolled his shoulders. 'And you just made a big mistake returning to our town, Tyler Coleman.'

The man chuckled, nothing in his calm demeanour suggesting that Jim's identification was correct, but his eyes gleamed, perhaps with real humour.

'And you've got the wrong man.' He placed his hands on the table and clasped them. 'So, leave.'

'And I reckon I'm right. So, you'll come with us.' Jim edged a pace to the side, leaving a clear route to the door.

With a flick of his head the man

glanced at each of the men lying on the floor beside him, then slid his hands to the edge of the table. He rocked forward, moving as if to rise, then slumped back into his chair and rested his hands on his lap.

'I assume that once I've proved who I am and that I'm not this . . . this Tyler Coleman, you'll release me.'

'*If* I've made a mistake, you can go. But now, you got yourself a choice — come with me and get the court's justice.' Jim raised his Peacemaker to sight the man's forehead. 'Or stay sitting and get my justice.'

The man leaned forward and rocked his head from side to side, but then twitched. Hot fire thundered up through the table as he ripped lead at the deputy from a concealed weapon. Splinters flew as the slug hurtled by Jim's ear and blasted into the ceiling.

Jim dived to the side, saving himself from a second slug. And Hopeman tore off a wild shot as the man kicked out. The toe of the man's boot hit the table and knocked it up into Hopeman's face, forcing the sheriff to waste another shot, firing blind.

As Hopeman extricated himself from the furniture, the man leapt to his feet and swung his gun round to aim at the sprawling deputy. In desperation, Hopeman lunged for his arm then thrust it high.

They struggled, both men straining to turn the derringer on the other man. Their mutual grip around the gun fired another slug into the ceiling, but by then Jim was on his feet. He waited for an opening and, when the man pushed Hopeman away, he sent him sprawling with a solid blow to the chin.

Even as the man was sliding to a halt, Jim was on him. He kicked his gun away, then hoisted him up by the collar and thrust the barrel of his gun right between his eyes.

'Assaulting a lawman,' he grunted, 'is another charge I can add to the list, Tyler Coleman.'

Even though the barrel forced the man's head back, he ignored the gun, his eyes only for the deputy.

'If you're so sure of who I am, shoot me.'

Jim snorted, then dragged him up to a sitting position.

'I ain't doing that. I reckon everyone in Clearwater should get a chance to see you swing.'

Hopeman yanked the man's arms back and secured him in handcuffs. Then, while he pulled their prisoner to his feet, Jim checked that the other men in the room were, in fact, dead.

Then he glanced through the window. Out on the road, passers-by had stopped and were peering up at the hotel room, but Jim didn't acknowledge them and went to the door. He checked that the corridor was clear, then, five paces ahead of Hopeman and their prisoner, left the hotel room and paced down the stairs into the Lucky Star saloon.

As Jim expected, the gunfire had

silenced the saloon's normally boister-ous evening crowd. Now the customers lined the bar, staring up the stairs at the three descending men with the wide-eyed bemusement that greeted the rare trouble that came Clearwater's way.

But then, at the end of the bar, Max Malloy muttered an oath and tipped back his hat. The people around him turned to ask what had surprised him, but Max's mouth just fell open and stayed open. Then he barged the men surrounding him aside and dashed out into the road, calling out the news.

So by the time Jim pushed the batwings apart all the people who had been out in the road were milling before the saloon and eager to see if Max was right.

But the gathering crowd parted as Hopeman dragged their uncomplaining prisoner to the sheriff's office. And, from the mutterings and the shaking heads, many of the people in the crowd, like Max, had recognized their prisoner.

As always, the undertaker, Gene

Trentham, was waiting on the board-walk outside the office, but for once his tall hat wasn't set at a jaunty angle in anticipation of business.

'Start smiling, Gene,' Hopeman said as Deputy Newell emerged from the office and opened the office door for him. 'You got two customers back in the Lucky Star. And this one will need your services soon.'

Gene flashed a wan smile, then lowered his head.

'I got more business than just that,' he murmured. 'It's Monty Elwood. And he's dead.'

With just a raised eyebrow, Hopeman ordered Jim to deal with this, then dragged the prisoner into the sheriff's office.

'How did he die?' Jim asked as the sheriff kicked the door shut behind him.

Gene hunched over, wringing his hands. A long sigh escaped his lips as he shuffled round on the spot, then led Jim through the thronging crowd and back across the road.

'It ain't much of a sight,' he murmured. 'He put a shotgun to his head.'

Jim snorted a humourless chuckle.

'Surprised his aim was good enough to hit anything he shot at.'

Gene returned an agreeing snort. 'Yeah, but from the empty whiskey bottle by his body, I reckon he was just drunk enough to kill himself, and just sober enough to do it right.'

'And you found him?'

'Yeah.' Gene stopped on the board-walk outside Monty's run-down store. 'I heard the gunfire in the Lucky Star and came to see what was happening, but then heard another gunshot in his store. So, I looked in on him. And . . . '

Jim rubbed his chin. 'Had you seen him earlier?'

'Yeah, in the Lucky Star. He was his usual self.' Gene considered Jim. 'What you thinking?'

'I'm just wondering if he'd seen that Tyler Coleman was back in town.'

Gene nodded as he pushed the door open.

'I guess that would have been enough to make him kill himself.'

Jim glanced over his shoulder at the sheriff's office where the townsfolk were now five deep around the windows and door, and craning their necks in hope of seeing the prisoner. He shrugged, then headed inside after Gene and paced across the store.

A smear of blood, a shotgun, and an empty whiskey bottle on the counter heralded what he would see, but Jim still took a deep breath before he glanced over the counter.

Monty lay sprawled on the floor, his lower leg bent and to the side, a hand outstretched as if reaching for something. But the thick pool of blood surrounding his head and the wasted remnants of his face said that he'd never reach whatever it was he was grasping for.

Jim and Gene stood with their heads bowed. Then Jim slipped behind the counter and stood over the body. He faced the door. The shotgun was at his right hand, the barrels aiming towards the door, and the whiskey bottle was at his left hand. He mimed taking the gun in hand, holding the barrels right between his eyes, and pulling the trigger.

He staggered back, then stood aside to look down at the body again. He judged that if Monty had shot himself, he would have fallen in the place where the body was now lying, and the shock would have driven the shotgun from his hand to let it spin to a halt on the counter.

He stepped over the body and came out from behind the counter. More spots of blood were on the counter and even on the floor beyond.

'You worried this wasn't suicide?' Gene asked.

Jim glanced over the counter at the body, then knelt to finger one of the blood spots. He shook his head.

'Our prisoner was busy getting

arrested when this happened. But as we can't ask Monty whether he saw Tyler before he killed himself, I'll note that he probably did, and put this death down as being Tyler's last victim.'

Gene nodded and together, they left the store. In silence, they parted and, as Gene headed to his workshop, Jim returned to the sheriff's office.

In the last five minutes the crowd had doubled in size. Everyone who had been in the Lucky Star had joined the others in a vigil outside the office. But as yet, the low conversation was more excited than annoyed as everyone shared the snippets of information they'd gathered.

Jim didn't expect the cheerful attitude to last for long.

He fought a path through the crowd, refusing all demands to add more details or confirm that the man they had arrested was, in fact, Tyler Coleman.

Nobody asked him about Monty Elwood.

Inside the office, he relayed the circumstances of Monty's death to Hopeman, receiving frequent sad shakes of the head from Hopeman in acknowledgement of the death of Clearwater's least reputable citizen.

But a firm and steady knock at the door halted Jim's tale.

They looked to the window, where outside, the crowd milled in, pressing their faces to the window. But one gaunt and tall man stood out from the rabble.

Everyone gave this man a wide berth, suggesting he was generating his own zone of quiet despair as he glared through the window in the door, his deep-set eyes lost to a sorrow that time could never heal.

Together, Hopeman and Jim winced.

'Caleb Lawson,' Hopeman murmured.

Jim sighed. 'Guessed it wouldn't be long before the news of Tyler's arrest spread to him. Shall I let him in?'

Hopeman sighed, then slapped his hands against his legs.

12

'Yeah. At the very least, we'll get an official identification.'

Jim nodded, then opened the door and stood before the doorway, his hands raised to grip the doorframe.

'Father,' he said, 'I'm obliged that you came.'

Caleb raised his chin, his back as straight as always, his eyes as cold as they had been for the last five years.

'I had to,' he muttered, his jaw set fit to burst. 'Now you've finally got the man who shot our Benny.'

'I hope it's him, but you can tell us for sure, if you can cope.'

'I can,' Caleb grunted. 'Stand aside.'

Jim kept a hand on the doorframe, blocking Caleb's route into the office, then held out his other hand and looked down at Caleb's gunbelt.

'Only when I have your gun.'

Caleb placed his hands on his hips. 'I won't shoot that snake. I want to savour the moment when the law finally delivers justice and he swings.'

'I know, Father, I know. That's why

we took him alive.' Jim flashed a smile. 'But you will give me your gun.'

'Your mother would never have accepted your treating me like that.' Caleb's jaw muscles rippled, but then, with a lunge, he unhooked his gunbelt and thrust it into Jim's hand. 'Now will you trust me?'

Jim rocked back to throw the belt on his desk. He decided that as he'd already insulted his father far more than he deserved, he wouldn't make it worse by frisking him for a hidden weapon. So he stood aside and directed him to the corner cell.

Caleb glanced over Jim's shoulder, receiving a ripple of dignified encouragement from the nearest people surrounding the door, then headed inside.

Several people tried to follow him in, but Jim stood before the door and, with a few polite pushes, removed them from the office, then closed the door. With his back to the door, he watched Caleb pace to a halt and glare

14

at the corner cell.

For long moments, the office was quiet. The prisoner sat on his bunk, staring through the bars at Caleb. Deputy Newell and Sheriff Hopeman stood on either side of Caleb, watching him snort long breaths through his nostrils. Caleb just stared at the prisoner, his eyes wide and blank.

Hopeman gestured to Jim, then to the windows. Seeing his concern, Jim closed the shutters, cutting off the view of the people outside of an encounter that nobody in Clearwater ever expected to see.

Jim's bustling activity broke Caleb's catatonic spell, and he strode towards the cell, then swung to a halt at arm's length from the bars.

'Got to ask you,' Hopeman said, 'is that him?'

Caleb slammed his eyes closed and gripped his hands so tightly all colour drained from them.

Hopeman and Jim exchanged a glance. Then Hopeman strode across the room and laid a hand on Caleb's shoulder.

This encouraged Caleb to open his eyes and look to the ceiling.

'That's Tyler Coleman,' he said, his voice a strangulated whisper, 'the man who shot my son.'

Inside the cell the prisoner uttered a snort, but Hopeman patted Caleb's shoulder and gently directed him away from the cell.

'I'll need more from you later, but for now, that will — '

Caleb pushed Hopeman away from him to stand clear and, with a trembling finger, pointed into the cell.

'Whatever you need to hang *that* man high, just ask. I'll do anything, go anywhere, pay anything. I'll . . . I'll . . . '

'Understood, Caleb, but you can rest easy now. It's over.'

'It ain't over.' Caleb raised his hand and rubbed it over his face, stilling the shaking. Then looked the prisoner up and down, his expression now more tired than shocked. 'I won't rest easy until he swings.'

Hopeman nodded and stood aside, letting Caleb head to the door.

Before the door, Caleb stomped to a halt, then, without looking at Jim, held out his hand.

Jim took the gunbelt from the desk and slapped it into Caleb's palm. Caleb moved to grab the door, but then glanced over his shoulder to look again at Tyler.

The prisoner had rolled from his bunk and stood. He'd thrown up both hands to grab the bars and pressed his face between them. He licked his lips and grinned.

Caleb's shoulders shook. His lips trembled as a solitary tear fell from his right eye. Then, with a huge roar, he swung round, aiming his gun while it was still in the holster at Tyler.

Jim saw Caleb's intent and lunged to the side to knock Caleb's arm up as he fired. Lead blasted through the bottom of the holster, but it clattered into the cell bars, a foot above Tyler's head.

As the slug ricocheted away, Tyler dived for cover beneath his bunk, but Jim grabbed Caleb's arm and held it high, and Hopeman prised the gun and gunbelt from his slack fingers.

'Father,' Jim said, 'that wasn't the way.'

'It's the only way that snake will understand,' Caleb roared.

Caleb flexed his shoulders and tried to push Jim and Hopeman from him, but the lawmen had a firm grip of his arms and swung him round and to the door.

'Hey,' Tyler whined, peering out from under his bunk, 'I want to press charges. He tried to kill me.'

'Be quiet, Tyler,' Hopeman shouted over his shoulder.

Deputy Newell opened the door. Outside, the crowd pressed in, but when Jim manoeuvred Caleb outside, Gene slipped through the people.

A wan smile from Jim was all the

explanation Gene needed as he led Caleb away.

Jim stood in the doorway. His firm-jawed stance and steady glaring encouraged the crowd to break up and wander back to their former business, shaking their heads.

Then he returned to the office, locked the door, and joined Hopeman and Newell in sitting at his desk in anticipation of what he was sure would be a long vigil.

'Don't want you to go thinking I ain't obliged, Deputy,' Tyler shouted from his cell. 'You just saved my life.'

'Only so you can swing,' Jim said.

'I wouldn't be so sure of that.' Tyler chuckled, then rolled on to his bunk. 'I reckon you'll live just long enough to regret that mistake.'

2

'You reckon anyone else will come?' Jim asked.

Gene glanced at the door to his workshop, then at Monty Elwood's coffin.

'I doubt it,' he said.

Jim and Hopeman glanced around Gene's workshop. Gene had set out two rows of chairs, but the two lawmen were the only people who had come to pay their respects.

They both sighed, then removed their hats.

It had been two days since they'd captured Tyler Coleman.

Tyler's murder of Benny Lawson five years earlier was still an open sore for many. So, in case anyone else decided to deliver justice to Clearwater's most notorious wanted man before Judge Plummer could come from Green

Valley, Hopeman and his deputies had remained on constant guard. But after Caleb's sudden action, nobody had tried anything.

Even so, there was a constant bustle of people outside the office, each person eager to see the prisoner.

So, with all that activity, the funeral of Monty Elwood had just been forgotten.

But in the quiet part of the afternoon Hopeman had left Deputy Newell in charge of guarding Tyler for an hour so that the two lawmen could attend the burial.

'Father Stanton must be coming, surely?' Hopeman asked, glancing around the unoccupied chairs.

Gene shook his head. 'He ain't coming either.'

'But he officiated over the burial of those two hired guns.'

Gene winced. 'Ever since Monty stole Stanton's cross and tried to sell it in his store, he's never forgiven him.'

Hopeman snorted. 'I thought religion

was all about forgiving.'

'It is, but I reckon everyone has a limit.'

'And Monty pushed those limits.' Hopeman blew out his cheeks. 'Well, if we ain't got a man of the cloth to say a few words, what do we do?'

'Monty wouldn't have wanted any Bible words uttered over his body. But I guess one of us ought to be able to say something about him.'

Gene looked at Hopeman, who snorted and looked away, then at Jim, but Jim took a deep breath and stood. So Gene made way for Jim to stand by the coffin. The deputy stared down at the lid, rocking his head from side to side, then turned to face Gene and Hopeman.

'Monty Elwood was . . . ' Jim shrugged and rubbed his chin. 'He was . . . He was a man.'

Hopeman chuckled. 'You got to say more than that.'

Jim slapped the coffin lid. 'Then I'll say this: He enjoyed life. He always had a kind word to say to you. And no matter how much mischief he caused, he never pushed things too far. So, I'll remember him as a decent citizen of Clearwater.'

For long moments silence reigned.

'Who are you talking about now?' Hopeman asked.

'Monty, he . . . ' Jim sighed on seeing that Hopeman was smiling.

'Sheriff,' Gene said, 'a man is dead, and even if that man is Monty Elwood, we must pay him some respect.'

'Only respect I can pay the likes of Monty Elwood is that Clearwater will be quieter without him. And you can take that any way you want.' Hopeman swung his hat on to his head and stood. 'Anybody else want to say something before we plant him in a hole?'

'I do,' a voice intoned from the doorway.

Everyone turned to see that a burly man was filling the doorway. A thick red beard covered his face almost up to the sharp eyes that were darting their gaze about the room, sizing up the few occupants within moments.

'Who are you?' Hopeman asked.

With slow paces the man strode into the room and stomped to a halt to stand with his legs planted wide. He removed his hat and batted the trail dust to the floor against his thigh, then ruffled his buffalo-hide jacket.

'Name's Armstrong McGiven. And I knew Monty Elwood.' He glanced at the coffin and closed his eyes for a moment. His lips mouthed something, perhaps a silent prayer. Then he strode across the room to stand beside the coffin. 'How did he die?'

'He shot himself,' Gene said.

Armstrong lowered his head. 'That ain't any kind of death for a man like Monty.'

'I guess you're right,' Hopeman murmured. He glanced at Jim and Gene with his eyebrows raised, but both men returned a bemused shrug.

Armstrong reached out to remove the

coffin lid, but Gene placed a hand on his arm.

'It's a mighty bad sight,' Gene said. 'He aimed real well.'

'I've seen dead men before.' Armstrong swung the lid away and peered down at Monty. He winced.

'I told you it was — '

'I ain't concerned about the sight. It's the smell.'

Gene leaned over the coffin and sniffed.

'Monty don't smell much worse dead than alive.'

Armstrong swung the lid back on the coffin.

'Then clean him up.'

'I don't see why . . . ' Gene glanced at Hopeman for support, but Armstrong extracted a wad of bills from his pocket, then peeled off a ten-dollar bill and passed it to Gene.

'Will this repay your trouble?'

'I guess it will,' Gene said. 'What do you want me to do?'

'A man like Monty shouldn't be

buried in those rags. He deserves to meet his maker in his best.'

'Those clothes *were* his best.'

'Then get some decent clothes on him,' Armstrong snapped, then softened his voice. 'Get him cleaned up. Then I'll bury him with dignity.'

Gene nodded, then held his hands before him and bowed his head.

'I'll see to it.'

Armstrong turned and paced across the room and, without even acknowledging the two lawmen, departed from the undertaker's workshop, leaving everyone glancing at each other.

'Now,' Hopeman said, 'that was unexpected.'

Jim stood. 'Makes me wonder whether we misjudged Monty. He couldn't have always been a whiskey hound.'

Hopeman grunted his disbelief, but Jim left the workshop, thoughtfully rubbing his chin.

On the boardwalk he glanced along the road until he saw Monty's friend walking towards the Lucky Star, his gait purposeful.

Hopeman joined Jim and, with Clearwater being quiet this afternoon, encouraged him to find out how Armstrong had come to know Monty. So, while Hopeman returned to the sheriff's office to resume his guarding of Tyler Coleman, Jim followed Armstrong down the road and into the saloon.

At the bar he stood beside Armstrong and although Armstrong didn't acknowledge him he attracted the bartender's attention first and ordered two whiskeys.

'Obliged,' Armstrong said, still staring straight ahead. He pushed Jim's money aside and threw some coins on the bar. 'But I'll pay. Monty wouldn't have wanted me to do anything else.'

Jim fingered his money, then nodded and pocketed his coins.

'You speak well of him.'

'I will always do that.'

Jim's drink arrived and he swirled the

whiskey in the glass before taking a gulp.

'How did you know him?'

'We rode together some years back.' Armstrong knocked back half his drink, then placed the glass back on the bar. 'I saw him from time to time since, but I hadn't realized that . . . '

For the first time, Armstrong glanced at Jim and frowned, the sun-baked wrinkles around his eyes ridging.

'That he'd fallen so far?'

'Yeah. I thought the whole town would have turned out to mourn the passing of such a great man.' Armstrong glanced around the saloon, his ear cocked to listen to the hubbub of chatter. 'I never expected everyone to be talking about some lowdown outlaw and that the only people to attend his funeral would be the people who had to attend.'

'I didn't have to. Monty didn't worry me as much as he annoyed others.'

'Glad to hear it.' Armstrong leaned on the bar and sipped his whiskey.

Jim considered his drink, then sighed.

'And it's a pity you couldn't have arrived a few days earlier. Meeting an old friend might have persuaded Monty to avoid doing what he did.'

'Perhaps. But Monty always knew his own mind. If he'd decided to kill himself, he'd do it no matter what anyone said.'

From the corner of his eye Jim glanced at Armstrong.

'The Monty you talk about doesn't sound like the man everyone in Clearwater knew over the last few years. If you're staying in town after you've buried him, I'd appreciate hearing about a different side to him.'

Armstrong lowered his glass, then poured himself and Jim another whiskey.

'As long as tales are still told about a man, that man ain't really dead.' He sighed. 'But I can't. I'm moving on once I've buried Monty.'

For a few minutes they stood in companionable silence, but with their conversation ending, Max Malloy sidled down the bar with a lively grin on his face.

'You here to bury Monty, you say?' he asked.

Jim flashed a warning glance at Max, but Armstrong was already turning his head to face him.

'I am.'

'Good,' Max said. He licked his lips. 'Just hope the worms don't get so annoyed with the smell that they throw him back.'

As Max's two drinking companions, Channing and Grange, guffawed at Max's poor attempt at wit, Armstrong placed his glass on the bar and swung round to confront Max.

'Monty was the best shot, the bravest man, and the finest friend any man could want. You'll take that back, or I'll pound your head into the wall until something gives.'

Max gulped and glanced away, but Channing and Grange muttered an oath, then strode down the bar to flank him. With their encouraging presence, Max stood tall.

'I ain't taking anything back about the likes of Monty.'

Armstrong rolled his shoulders, but Jim slapped a firm hand on his arm.

'Deputy,' Armstrong said, glancing at the hand, 'you can't stop me from defending my friend's good name.'

'I wasn't. I was offering to help you.'

'Obliged for the offer, but I don't need no help to deal with these men.'

Max grunted his irritation and, with Channing and Grange goading him on, took a long pace towards Armstrong then hurled a flailing blow at his face. But Armstrong swayed back from the blow, then thudded a short-arm jab into Max's guts that bent him double.

As Max gasped for air, Armstrong grabbed his shoulders, turned him round, and kicked him towards his companions. Channing danced back, standing tall by the bar, and Max stumbled by him to crash into Grange.

The entangled men tumbled to the floor.

Grange watched them flounder, then turned, but walked into Armstrong's pile-driving blow to the jaw. His head cracked back as he toppled into the bar, but a second backhanded slap almost knocked him to his knees, only a sharp uppercut to his chin stopping him from falling. Then a solid slug to the cheek wheeled him over the bar.

As Grange clattered to the floor, Armstrong batted his hands together, but before he could turn, Channing extricated himself from Max. He rolled to his feet and leapt on Armstrong's back, then wrapped both hands around his chin and tried to yank his head back. But Armstrong merely dropped to his knees and thrust his head down to hurl Channing over his shoulders.

Channing somersaulted before he landed flat on his back, then sat up to meet a round-footed kick to the chin that pole-axed him in a moment.

Armstrong stood tall, then turned

and grabbed Max's collar and pulled him up to his chin. He glanced at the wall then at Max.

'Now, it's your turn,' he said, smiling. 'You want driven through that wall, or do you want to tell me what you really think of Monty?'

'Monty was a . . . was a . . . ' Max sighed and slumped his shoulders. 'He was a great man.'

With mock care, Armstrong patted Max's head.

'Now, whenever you see someone, you'll be sure to tell them that, won't you?'

'Yeah,' Max murmured.

Armstrong pulled Max to his feet and drew back his fist.

'That wasn't convincing enough!'

'He was a great man,' Max bleated.

'That *was* convincing.' Armstrong moved to kick Max a pace towards the door, but Jim pushed himself from the bar to stand beside them.

'That's enough,' he said. 'You've won this fight and now you've got no reason to kick Monty out of the saloon.'

Armstrong glanced at Jim, but then gave a begrudging nod.

'Apologies, Deputy,' he said as, with a snap of his wrist, he released Max's collar.

Jim nodded, then grabbed Max's jacket and marched him to the door. With a firm lunge he hurled him through the batwings. He watched Max roll off the boardwalk to lie on his back in the road, then returned to the bar.

'Apology accepted,' he said. 'Just remember it's my job to throw his sort out of saloons.'

Armstrong nodded his approval while filling Jim's half-full whiskey glass.

Jim raised the glass to his lips, but noticed that behind him the hubbub of chatter in the saloon hadn't returned. As he lowered the glass, he also heard the doors creak and footfalls stomp into the saloon.

Jim glanced over his shoulder, expecting Max to have returned to escalate his fight, but a squat man stood with a hand on each batwing, peering around the saloon with his hat cocked low and his gaze cold. Out on the boardwalk three other men flanked him.

His rolling gaze centred on Jim. A sneering snort escaped his thin lips. Then, to his beckoning wave, all four men swaggered into the saloon and straight towards Jim.

3

The men brushed past Jim and lined up at the bar beside him.

Jim turned and fingered his glass, but when the bartender provided the newcomers with whiskeys, Jim felt the back of his neck burn. He still stayed hunched, but when the feeling refused to go away, with a deliberate swing of the head he turned.

The man who had entered the saloon first was looking at him.

Jim tipped back his hat. 'You want me?'

'Yeah,' the man murmured through clenched teeth. 'I was heading to the sheriff's office to give Sheriff Hopeman a message. But you can save me a journey.'

'And the message?'

'He'll release Tyler Coleman by sundown, if he doesn't want trouble from Luther Wade.'

Jim pushed himself from the bar and swung round to confront the man, Luther.

'A man who provides messages like that is looking to join Tyler in a cell.'

Luther shrugged and hunched over the bar. Beside him, the other three men drank their whiskeys with the studied intensity of men who were making a show of ignoring this conversation.

Luther raised his glass to his lips, but then lowered it.

'I ain't done nothing wrong, Deputy.'

'Yet,' Jim muttered squaring off to Luther. 'But words are easy. You got the guts to deliver more?'

Luther fingered his glass, then pushed it away from him, swirling the liquid across the bar. He turned to look Jim up and down, then snorted.

'I'll bide my time.' Luther took a steady pace towards Jim. 'But if Tyler is still in a cell at sundown, I'll do what I have to do.'

Jim bent at the waist to thrust his face into Luther's face, their noses just inches apart.

'Now, that was a threat. And men who make threats end up in a cell.'

With his index finger, Luther tipped his hat back on his head, then patted that finger against his bristled chin as he backed away a pace, a smile twitching his lips.

'And men who don't heed my warnings end up in a hole. You got until sundown.'

Jim sneered. 'I was right about you the first time I saw you. You're a yellow-belly.'

Luther's right eye twitched. He bunched a fist but when Jim looked him up and down and chuckled he slackened his hand and swung round to move towards the door.

But then he snapped back, his hand whirling to his holster.

Jim had anticipated Luther's action and went for his gun. But Armstrong lunged out from the bar and grabbed

Luther's wrist as the fingers brushed the stock, then pulled the hand high.

'Run along,' he murmured, thrusting the arm up Luther's back and spinning him round, 'like the deputy told you.'

The men at the bar edged back a pace, their hands twitching towards their gunbelts, but a shake of the head from Luther made them raise their hands.

Armstrong held on to Luther, but when Luther grunted an oath, he thrust his arm up so that Luther had to stand on tiptoes, then pushed him towards the door.

Luther stumbled to a halt, but he remained facing the door. Then, with a roll of the shoulders and a smoothing of his jacket, he paced across the saloon. A short wave encouraged the other men to peel from the bar.

With Luther at the back, the men strode to the saloon door, each pace slow and deliberate, the gaze of everyone in the saloon on them, but Luther stopped in the doorway.

'I'm leaving,' he said, looking into the road, 'but only because I chose to. Next time, I'll leave with Tyler Coleman.'

Then, with a sideways glare at Jim and a mocking tip of his hat, Luther paced through the batwings and outside.

★ ★ ★

'We got trouble,' Jim said as he walked into the sheriff's office. 'Luther Wade is back in town.'

'Who's he?' Newell asked.

'Five years ago he roared through Clearwater with Tyler Coleman. Tyler had the brains. Luther had the gun.'

Hopeman looked up from his desk, nodding.

'Where did you see him?' he asked.

'He was in the saloon with three other hard-cases threatening to break Tyler out of jail by sundown.'

Hopeman glanced to the corner cell, but Tyler was just as morose as he had been since they'd arrested him.

He didn't look up.

'Recognize them?'

'Recognized the type, but not the men.'

Hopeman drew Jim to the window and out of Tyler's earshot.

'Luther will have more men with him than that. Later, they'll ride into town and bide their time as they wait for Luther to make his move.'

'Then things are looking bad.'

'Not all bad. I'm comforted to know Tyler's friend wants him out.'

'What you mean?'

Hopeman lowered his voice. 'Judge Plummer should be here within the week for Tyler's trial, but I'm worried what'll happen then. I've been pulling together the evidence and I got to admit there's no real proof that Tyler killed your brother.'

'But he did,' Jim snapped.

'I know, but Monty was the only witness.'

Jim tipped back his hat. 'Are you saying someone killed Monty to stop him testifying? Because it looked to me like he killed himself.'

'I don't know what to believe. Gene is the only one who's sure he heard a gunshot in Monty's store. Some reckon they might have heard a shot an hour earlier, but — '

'That ain't enough to doubt anything.'

'It ain't.' Hopeman paced round on the spot, tapping a fist against his thigh, then looked at Jim. 'But there's more happening here than I first thought. I've alerted Marshal Kirby, but as I don't want to call him in, it's time we found some real proof.'

★   ★   ★

Jim stood in the doorway to Monty's store, his lip curled with distaste. With Jim's interest in forming a case against Tyler Coleman being so personal, Sheriff Hopeman had let him take control of the investigation, and his first discovery was that someone had ransacked the place.

After the saloon fight, he assumed that it was Max Malloy and, from the systematic nature of the destruction, he reckoned Max was looking for something.

So, Jim left the store and asked around, learning that Max had hurried out of town, heading west towards Black Pass. This was just too much of a coincidence, so, at a gallop, Jim rode out of Clearwater, but he glanced all around him as he kept on the look-out for Luther Wade.

But only when he closed on the small rounded hill at the junction of the trails north and west did he see the first movement out on the trail.

He narrowed his eyes and confirmed that it was just Gene Trentham's wagon. And when he was closer he saw that riding up front with Gene was Armstrong McGiven and that on the back sat a simple wooden coffin.

Jim slowed to avoid disrupting their dignified journey to the town cemetery.

But with the wagon travelling painfully slowly, Jim had no choice but to be just a few dozen yards behind them when the wagon pulled up.

He watched Gene and Armstrong alight and slide the coffin from the back of the wagon. Gene nodded towards him, but Armstrong didn't look at him.

Jim waited until they were walking up the hill, then hurried his horse on, but as he passed the wagon, he slowed to a halt.

His journey was pressing, but after being a party to the rude way they'd dealt with Monty's funeral earlier today, he decided to make amends by paying his respects properly.

Still, he didn't join them, but dismounted and stood at the base of the hill. With his hat removed, he watched Armstrong and Gene carry the coffin to the brow of the hill.

They lowered the coffin into the ground and immediately Gene turned and headed down the hill, leaving Armstrong to cover the hole with rocks on his own.

Gene smiled at Jim as he passed and confirmed he would be welcome, so he paced up the hill and joined Armstrong.

'This is a good place,' he said, halting ten yards back from Armstrong.

Armstrong looked up, his jaw set firm. 'It is.'

'When you've gone, I'll pass by and tend Monty's grave.'

'Why?'

Jim opened his mouth, then closed it. He rejected several answers before settling for the truth.

'You stood by me in the saloon when Luther Wade was getting gun-crazy, and my mother and Benny are buried just down the hill, so it's no trouble.'

Armstrong shrugged. 'I don't want you helping if you think Monty was a worthless varmint like Max and everybody else in Clearwater does.'

Jim joined Armstrong and stared down at the small mound of stones.

'I don't think that no more. The way

you defended his memory gave me a hint of the man Monty once was. I reckon now that he was a decent man, who caused no harm to anyone. Then he just happened to be with my brother when Tyler killed him and his life spiralled downwards.'

Armstrong nodded and knelt to pick up another stone.

'It did at that.'

Jim placed a hand over his heart. 'I, for one, will never speak ill of Monty Elwood.'

'Then, perhaps my work here ain't done.' Armstrong placed the stone on the pile and reached for another. 'If I can help one man to accept that Monty was decent, I reckon I'll stay until I can persuade another man to come here and pay his respects.'

'If you're staying that long, I'll . . . ' Jim bit back the rest of his ill-considered comment, but Armstrong looked up at him, smiling.

'If that was going to be a bad joke, don't worry. Monty had a sense of humour. He'd have laughed.' Armstrong removed the smile, then hefted the stone and slammed it down. 'Now leave me. I have a friend to bury.'

Jim nodded and left Armstrong. He paced down the hill, but half-way down, he veered off to stand before a neat and familiar grave.

'Mother,' he said, looking towards Black Pass, 'I've arrested the man who I reckon killed our Benny. I hope that'll put Father out of his torment. But I know you wouldn't want me to condemn an innocent man, so I got a lot of investigating to do first. Either way, when I've found out the truth, I'll tell you about it. And this time, I promise I'll get Father to come and see you, too.'

And with that promise made, Jim stood aside to glance at Benny's grave. He gave a short nod, then swung his hat on his head and strode down the hill to his horse.

He'd lost time and, with sundown only a few hours away, he didn't want to risk being late for Luther's threatened return. But he still headed on a wide arc around the outskirts of his father's ranch until he reached Black Pass.

The pass was ten miles to the south of Devil's Canyon and was just a short pass on the western route to Green Valley.

Jim rode into the pass and pulled his horse to a halt at the point where the sides were at their steepest. A solitary tree stood there, the strain of being so close to the spot where Benny died probably helping to bow its branches. He dismounted and turned on the spot, glancing at the rugged sides of the pass.

After so many years he didn't expect to see anything interesting, but as most people avoided the pass, Jim included, familiarizing himself with this place felt the right thing to do before he resumed his search for Max.

He looked up the slope at his side, seeing plenty of places where a man could hide out and fire a fatal shot at someone at the bottom of the pass. He considered scouting around, but instead, mounted his horse and paced it in a short circle, ensuring this deserted place embedded itself in his mind.

But then the thought of just how few people headed through the pass returned to Jim.

He glanced towards the western end of the pass. Five miles beyond was Bart Haley's ranch, and this man had ranched here for many years. And with his solitary ways, Jim doubted that Hopeman had questioned him.

With a hand to his brow, Jim considered the sun, which, as he looked, dipped below the side of the pass. He shrugged, then turned his horse to the pass's western exit.

But as he rounded the corner seven riders swung into view. One of the men was Max Malloy, and they were peering around the pass in the same way that Jim had been doing. On seeing Jim they swung round to face him.

Jim pulled his horse to a halt.

'Max Malloy,' he shouted, 'I've been looking for you.'

Max glared back at him, then drew his gun and fired. The shot flew way over Jim's head, but the other men joined Max in firing.

Jim pulled his horse round on the spot and galloped around the corner. Gunfire from behind hurried him on his way.

But then, from ahead, two more riders appeared, galloping towards him along the pass. And just as Jim recognized them as being Channing and Grange, they blasted a volley of gunfire that tore through the air around him.

4

Jim flinched as another gunshot whistled by his ear.

As the crisp crack of gunfire echoed around him, he glanced left and right, weighing up his prospects of reaching either end of the pass against holding up.

But Channing blasted a rapid burst of gunfire into the dirt before his horse and resolved his problem for him.

So, he turned his horse to the right and headed past the steepest part of the pass and on to a huge rocky outcrop.

Under an overhang, he leapt down from his horse and hunkered down behind a boulder that covered him from view from either side of the pass.

He bobbed up and saw Channing and Grange shuffle down behind a boulder on the other side of the trail, forty yards away and ten yards from the pass bottom.

Other movement rippled to their side as at least one other man scurried for cover.

'Ambushing a lawman is a big mistake,' Jim shouted. His voice echoed back at him from the other side of the pass.

Jim waited for one of the men to shout back, hoping to gather some clues as to where the remaining men had gone to ground, but they remained silent.

On hands and knees he crawled to the side of the boulder and peered around, but a gunshot ripped into the earth beside his hand, forcing him to scurry back for cover.

'You're facing a heap of trouble for this,' he shouted.

Jim crawled to the other side of the boulder to peer in the other direction, but a gunshot winged into the boulder, ripping shards into his face.

He reckoned that with the pass sides being so steep, any attempt to climb to safety would expose him for far too long. So, on his belly, Jim snaked to his horse, the boulder at least giving him cover to get under the overhang without his attackers being able to see him.

He stood and glanced along the length of the overhang, but it was only thirty feet wide and, on either side, the overhang had fallen away, leaving no cover between him and his attackers.

As Jim debated mounting his horse and running for it he saw, on the other side of the pass, the slash of darkness rise as the sun headed for the horizon. And even as he looked, that shadow climbed ever higher up the pass.

Luther had promised to come for Tyler at sundown, and Jim reckoned he was a man who kept his promises. So, even though Max had pinned him down, he had to find a way out. Jim dropped to his knees and crawled towards the covering boulder.

But then pebbles drizzled to the ground before him.

He just had time to realize they'd

fallen from the edge of the overhang when a man dropped from above, landing lightly, but still stumbling to the side.

Jim didn't give the man time to regain his footing, he jumped to his feet then pounded across the ground towards him.

On the run, he had time to blast one wild gunshot at the man. Then he hit him full in the side and knocked him back three paces before both men tumbled to the ground.

Jim's Peacemaker fell from his hand, but he landed on top of the man, lifted himself high, then slugged the man's jaw. His opponent shrugged off the blow and bucked him from his chest. But Jim had a firm grip of the man's arms and the two men rolled to the side, struggling to throw punches at each other from such close quarters.

Jim realized that they'd rolled out from the overhang and were now in full view of the men on the other side of the pass. So he clung on to his opponent, not giving them a clear shot at him.

With each man clutching hold of the other's arms as they tried to wrestle each other down, they rolled one way, then the other, dust pluming up around them.

Then gunfire blasted in the pass, echoing as it seemingly exploded from more than one position. This surprised his opponent as much as it did Jim, and the grip on Jim's arms lessened as the man glanced up to see who had been foolish enough to fire at them when they were so entangled.

Jim took advantage of his opponent's distraction to release his own hold then slug his jaw.

The man's head cracked back but Jim kept hold of him, then rolled over him and grabbed him from behind. He climbed to his feet and placed the man's back to him, using him as a human shield.

Gunfire rippled down the pass again, but this time Jim realized that none of it was directed at him and that it was all coming from further down the pass.

Then a lone rider emerged around the long arc, galloping straight for his position.

Jim smiled on recognizing the newcomer as Armstrong, then pulled the man's gun from its holster and fired up at the opposite side of the pass, aiming for his attackers' position and forcing them to stay down.

But with Jim's attention wavering, the man used the opportunity to yank his arms free of Jim's grasp and launch a fist backhanded at Jim's chin. Jim hurled up his arm and deflected the blow with his forearm, then swung his gun up and slugged the man's temple with the cold metal.

But the man rolled with the blow and fell to his knees. He knelt with his head lolling, then launched himself to his feet as he ripped a knife from his boot.

Jim darted his head back, saving himself from the man's wild slash. And, as the man thrust his arm forward, aiming to stab him in the belly, Jim fired a low slug that tore into the man's guts. The man still staggered on a half-pace, momentum dragging the knife onward, but Jim fired again, rocking the man back on his heels before he keeled over on to his back.

Jim turned at the hip and fired two speculative shots at the other side of the pass, then collected his own gun from the ground and scurried for his horse. In a lithe action he leapt on it and dragged it out from the overhang.

With Armstrong standing square in the middle of the pass and laying down covering fire, he hurried away from the overhang and down the pass, firing over his shoulder. The echoes made the gunfire sound far more intense than just two men could make.

Armstrong saw his intent and fired one last volley, then dragged his horse round on the spot, the horse prancing for a moment before he got it under control, and hurtled for the western end of the pass.

One of the attackers made the

mistake of straying out from his cover and Jim blasted this man through the chest. This encouraged the other men to stay down, so he thrust the gun in his belt and concentrated on putting distance between the attackers and himself, but as he reached the exit, he slowed to let Armstrong draw alongside him.

But a glance over his shoulder confirmed that five men were now in pursuit. They closed: 300 yards, 200, 100, and Armstrong's and Jim's tired horses were slowing with every pace.

Jim reloaded both his guns and, when the leading horse was thirty yards behind him, he swung round in the saddle and fired.

Armstrong joined him and they laid down an arc of deadly gunfire that ripped into the closest man, knocking him from his horse, his trailing foot catching and letting him be dragged along behind his steed.

Gunfire whistled past Jim's head, but he took careful aim at the next nearest man and fired. He wasted three shots, but the fourth grazed the man's shoulder, forcing him to throw up a hand to clutch his wounded shoulder. A second shot wheeled him to the ground.

As Max hurtled on to pass the dying man, 200 yards back from him, Channing and Grange galloped out from the pass.

Jim holstered his Peacemaker and thrust the other gun into his belt then, with a great roar and a slap of his hand on his horse's rump, tried to drag a last burst of speed from his steed.

At his side Armstrong did the same and they'd increased the gap to 200 yards by the time he looked back again.

Jim whooped his delight, but then realized that the increased distance was because Max was slowing. He exchanged a glance with Armstrong, hoping he'd offer a reason, but Armstrong shrugged.

Jim put a hand to his brow and saw that the men who had emerged from the pass had slowed to a halt and were milling in a circle. Max was gesturing to them, urging them to join the chase, but these men were gesturing back and not moving out on to the plains.

Jim didn't wait around to worry about the problems Max was having controlling these men and returned to concentrating on his riding.

And when he looked back after another quarter-mile, Max had stopped.

Both Jim and Armstrong whooped some more. Then Jim pointed forwards at Bart's ranch, some three miles away.

Armstrong grunted his agreement, then hurried his horse on. The two men galloped towards the ranch, and when Jim looked back again, Max had disappeared into the heat haze behind them.

This encouraged the two men to slow their horses to a trot and, with their safety now assured, Jim turned in the saddle to face Armstrong.

'Much obliged to you for helping me out — again.'

'No problem for someone who attended Monty's funeral,' Armstrong said.

Jim rode on for another minute before he spoke again.

'When you rescued me, you laid down so much gunfire, I thought for a moment I had more than one rescuer.'

Armstrong shrugged. 'It must have been the echoes.'

Jim nodded. 'It must have.'

With Jim in the lead, they rode on to Bart's land. The rough corral and unkempt wagon showed Bart's lack of interest in any activity beyond earning himself enough to live on. As Bart only ever came into Clearwater to trade and gained no friends with his surly attitude, Jim stopped twenty yards from the front of the small ranch house and waited for him to emerge.

Jim was just beginning to think that Bart wasn't here when the grizzled man paced through his door. And, as Jim had expected, he had a rifle levelled on them.

'That's far enough,' he grunted.

Jim raised his hands. 'It's Deputy Jim Lawson from Clearwater.'

'Don't care who you are.' Bart swung to the side to spit on the ground. 'You ain't staying on my land.'

'I don't aim to stay. I just got a question to ask.'

'I ain't done nothing but keep myself to myself.'

'I know. My question is whether you saw anyone come out of the pass.'

Bart bunched his bristled jaw as he stared at Jim, then provided a short shrug.

'Up until now, nope.'

'I'm not interested in what you saw today. I mean five years ago.'

'Five years! You've come here to ask me what I saw five years ago?' Bart watched Jim nod. Then, with a shake of his head, he swung the rifle over his shoulder and tipped back his hat. 'Then I guess you'd better ask that question.'

Jim nudged his horse forward to

stand before Bart. Armstrong stayed back.

'It was after my brother, Benny Lawson, died in the pass. Whoever killed him must have headed west afterwards and that meant they'd have passed your land. And I reckon nobody passes here that you don't notice.'

'You reckon right.' Bart strode out from his house to stand beside Jim's horse and peer towards the pass, his eyes glazing as he appeared to drag up an old memory. 'I saw your father leading a posse, and I'll tell you what I told him.' Bart looked up. 'I saw nothing.'

Jim sighed. 'Then I'll leave you. Obliged for your help.'

Jim turned his horse, aiming to join Armstrong, but Bart raised a hand, halting him.

'You didn't listen to what I said.' Bart raised his eyebrows, then provided a slow wink. 'I saw nothing.'

'Nothing is nothing.'

'It ain't, because like you say, I see

everyone that leaves the pass.' Bart pointed over Jim's left shoulder. 'Just like I can see those riders heading this way.'

Jim winced and glanced back. It was to see that Max was leading a line of four riders towards the ranch.

And they were galloping towards them brandishing their guns.

5

'You letting us in your house?' Armstrong said.

Bart glanced at the approaching riders, then provided a reluctant beckoning wave. So Armstrong and Jim corralled their horses, then dashed into the house. Bart stayed in the doorway.

Jim urged Bart to follow them in, but Bart shook his head and trained his rifle on the riders.

Through the window Jim watched Max pull his horse to a halt and glare down at Bart.

'Move aside,' Max grunted. 'We got business with the deputy.'

Bart firmed his rifle against his shoulder and sighted Max.

'You're on my land and unless you want to stay on it permanently, leave now.'

Max glanced at the windows, sharing

eye-contact with Armstrong and Jim, then shrugged and tugged on the reins. The flanking men moved to follow him, but then Channing and Grange swung their horses round and charged for the house.

Bart blasted at Max, but the man was already leaping from his horse and the lead hurtled over his form. But before Bart could swing round to fire at the other men, simultaneous slugs hammered into his chest from two different directions. He staggered back to crash to the floor, then moved to sit up as Jim dashed to his side to drag him into the house. But another slug ripped into his chest and forced Jim to flinch back.

By the side of the door Jim glanced at the bullet-ridden body, then shook his head and joined Armstrong at the window.

Outside, Max was taking cover behind the water-trough. Channing and Grange had dismounted and were dashing around the back of the house. Armstrong hurried the other two men into a hollow with a quick burst of gunfire, then darted back from the window as Max returned fire.

As Armstrong and Max traded shots, Jim glanced over his shoulder, confirming the door and window at the front were the only way in, then joined Armstrong in firing through the window.

One man bobbed up, but before he could fire, Armstrong planted a slug in his chest. And when Channing and Grange returned and scurried behind Bart's wagon, another man jumped up to cover them, but earned a slug in the neck for his trouble.

After this, Max urged caution and for the next half-hour the men inside and outside traded gunfire. But with Max not taking any risks, none of his men gained any positions closer to the house.

In a lull, Jim dragged Bart's body further into the house, then rejoined Armstrong at the window.

'Max,' he shouted, 'why did you

ransack Monty's store?'

'I ain't got to explain myself to you,' Max shouted.

'You'll explain either here or in a cell.'

'I won't. A snooping lawman like you ain't leaving here alive.' Max leapt up to fire at the house, then ducked.

'This is wrong,' Armstrong said. 'Monty had nothing worth stealing.'

'Perhaps he was looking for something, like he was looking for something in the pass.' Jim glanced at Bart's body. 'And either way, Max has silenced a potential witness to my brother's murder and, to me, that's mighty suspicious.'

Armstrong nodded, fingering his beard. 'How did your brother die?'

'I wasn't much involved at the time.' Jim glanced away. 'I was . . . I was distracted when it happened. But in short, Sheriff Hopeman ran Luther Wade out of town. His friend, Tyler Coleman, still loitered nearby and people said he came into town and thieved a-plenty. Then Tyler stole two thousand dollars from my father's ranch. A posse headed off after him.'

'And Benny was in the posse?'

'Nope. Benny was sixteen and eager to join the chase, but my father wouldn't let him. But Benny had the kind of enthusiasm that can make a man great, or will just get him killed.'

The two men stood in silence, each roving their gazes across the wagon and the water-trough.

'Gene said that Benny would have been a lawman one day.'

'He would,' Jim said, nodding. 'Benny had the instincts, and this was his chance to prove it. He asked around and something Monty said suggested to him that everyone had headed in the wrong direction.'

Outside, Max ventured a glance over the water-trough, but Armstrong blasted a shot over the trough that forced him to duck.

'What hint?'

'No idea. Anyhow, he deputized

Monty.' Jim chuckled. 'He had no right to do that, but Benny was the kind of man who naturally gave orders. So, they headed off in the opposite direction to the posse. But in Black Pass, the snake ambushed them.'

'Tyler Coleman?'

Jim firmed his jaw, then nodded. 'It couldn't be anyone else. Max Malloy followed them into the pass, but when he arrived the shooting was all over.'

'He was already dead?'

'Yeah. He'd only been shot in the leg, but he'd bled to death. Monty was sitting hunched beside the body and mumbling that he couldn't stop the bleeding. And Tyler was long gone, and so was the money.'

'If Tyler killed Benny, he must have been vicious to get past Monty.'

'That's as maybe, but my father wasn't in no mood for hearing excuses. He searched everywhere, but found no sign of Tyler.'

'And after the trail went cold?'

'Nothing.' Jim blasted a shot at

Channing who was daring to edge out from the wagon. 'The murder remained unsolved. Monty turned to the whiskey, my mother pined away and died, and my father and me have struggled to share a civil word since.'

'Your father blamed you for not catching Tyler?'

'Yeah. He reckoned there was no point having a lawman for a son if that lawman couldn't catch his brother's killer.' Jim sighed. 'And he's right.'

As Armstrong shrugged a huge burst of gunfire ripped out from outside, peppering the window and forcing them to duck.

When Jim risked glancing up it was to see that Grange and Channing were dashing for the door. He fired at them, but the two men gained a position pressed flat on either side of the door.

Then Grange kicked open the door. Jim swung out from the window and hammered gunfire through the open doorway, then waited for one of the men to make the mistake of trying to come through the door.

Long minutes passed with the door swaying in the breeze. Then Max fired at the window from outside, forcing Armstrong to return fire. With their forces distracted, Channing leapt through the doorway, running with his head thrust low.

Jim fired. The shot whistled over Channing's head, but Channing was bent so double that he tumbled himself to the floor. He skidded on his shoulder and while still moving, fired up.

The shot hurtled by Jim's nose and tore into the roof, but this gave Jim enough time to steady his stance and blast down at Channing. His shot thundered into his chest and flattened him, but even as he was firing a second time, Grange charged through the doorway.

Jim leapt to the side to avoid Grange's blast of gunfire, but Armstrong swung from the window and hammered a shot into Grange's back that buckled him almost to his knees. But Grange still staggered two paces, then fell into the crouched Jim.

From so close he entangled himself in Jim's limbs. Elsewhere in the house more gunfire sounded, but Jim had no choice but to ignore it and concentrate on bundling Grange away from him.

With a mixture of elbows and fists, he knocked Grange to the floor. But Grange, with one last desperate lunge, pulled his gun around to aim it at Jim, and Jim had no choice but to blast him between the eyes. Then he turned. Beside the door, Armstrong and Max were struggling.

Each clutched the other's wrist as they tried to wrestle Armstrong's gun down to aim it at the other man. But Jim rolled to his feet and stood by the door, then, with his back to the wall, watched the two men fight.

Max saw that he was now outnumbered and swung Armstrong round so that Armstrong stood between him and Jim and, with surprising strength, pulled the gun down inch by inch, turning it inexorably towards Armstrong's head. He risked one wild shot, the blast close enough to tear Armstrong's hat from his head.

Jim edged to the side, looking for an opening, but he couldn't get a clear shot at Max.

'To the ground,' Jim shouted.

At first Armstrong ignored the shouted plea, but then flinched and released Max's arm. He dropped. Even before he'd hit the floor Jim had fired two shots into Max's chest that wheeled him round to crash into the wall, then slide down it to lie on his front.

From the floor Armstrong nodded his thanks, then dashed around the fallen men in the house, checking they were dead.

But when he turned Max over he discovered that he was still breathing. He gestured for Jim to join him.

Jim hunkered down beside Max and shook his shoulders. Max's eyes rolled before they centred on Jim's face.

'Why?' Jim asked.

'I got my reasons,' Max murmured, his voice faint and broken.

'You're a troublemaker, but ambushing a lawman ain't like you.'

'I guess it wasn't,' Max murmured, his voice fading with every word. 'But I wasn't after you. I was after Monty Elwood.'

Jim glanced at Armstrong, who returned a shrug.

'You talking about five years ago?'

Max twitched. Pain contorted his face. Then he thrust up a hand to grab Jim's jacket and lever himself up a foot.

'I figured out where Monty was hiding and was all set to stop him talking. Then you arrived.' Max's grip loosened and he fell back to lie on the floor. 'But I guess Luther Wade will just have to . . .'

Jim shook Max's shoulder, but when his head lolled, he rolled back on his haunches to look up at Armstrong, who returned an expression that was as bemused as Jim felt.

'I guess he was confused at the end,'

Armstrong said, 'and couldn't work out the difference between today and five years ago.'

'I guess.'

With nothing else to accomplish at the ranch, Armstrong and Jim left the house. But as they headed to the corral, Jim pointed at the lengthening shadows, so, in short order, the two men mounted their horses and headed back to Black Pass at a gallop.

Just in case Max had had any more help they kept on their guard as they rode through the pass. But no more surprises came and in good time they left the pass and hurried on to Clearwater.

But by the time the town appeared ahead their horses were straining and they had no choice but to slow to a trot.

'You going to tell me who she was?' Armstrong asked.

Jim rode on with his jaw set firm, but then glanced to the side.

'She?'

'Yeah,' Armstrong said with subdued

laughter in his voice. 'When Tyler killed your brother, you were too *distracted* to be much involved. And to me, that means there was a woman involved.'

'I guess there was.' Jim sighed. 'Her name was Zelma.'

Armstrong snorted a deep breath, his eyes flaring for a moment.

'Zelma Hayden,' he murmured.

'You know her?'

'I know *of* her. Monty once said she was a mighty fine-looking woman.'

'She sure was, and we were close. I always assumed we were to wed.'

'Assumed?'

Jim leaned forwards in the saddle, shaking his head, but then pulled his horse to the side to ride alongside Armstrong.

'Yeah. I've had five years to wonder where I went wrong and I can now see that making too many assumptions was my problem. Zelma dreamt of seeing the world; I just wanted to be a lawman in Clearwater. I thought her fancy thoughts would fly away, but one day it

77

was she who flew.'

'She say why?'

'Nope. I tried to find her. Some people said she met a travelling salesman and went off with him. Some people saw this man, but more people didn't.' Jim sighed and slapped his thigh. 'So, the only thing I knew for sure was that she'd gone and she wasn't coming back.'

Armstrong chuckled with companionable laughter.

'That sure is a sad story.'

Jim returned a chuckle. 'Ain't it just.'

Armstrong rode on, but as he approached the first buildings on the outskirts of Clearwater he coughed and glanced at Jim.

'And this happened when Benny died?'

'Yeah.'

'And you got no reason to suppose her disappearance had anything to do with his murder?'

'No.' Jim narrowed his eyes. 'What you thinking?'

'Nothing.' Armstrong turned his horse to ride down the main road. 'I'm just trying to understand what happened.'

'Then tell me what you're — '

Gunfire blasted out from Clearwater's main road.

Jim glanced at the setting sun, then at Armstrong, who returned a wince, and the two men broke into a gallop.

6

When Clearwater's main road swung into view, Jim saw what he feared.

Strung out across the road a line of riders was circling before the sheriff's office, firing high and hollering, ensuring everyone knew they'd arrived. Luther Wade was in their midst and the rest of the men had the arrogant postures and trigger-happy attitudes of men hired to cause trouble.

At the end of the road Jim dismounted and, with Armstrong at his heels, dashed for the nearest cover, a row of barrels outside the hardware store. Then, he bobbed up and reviewed the situation.

Several of Luther's men were taking positions opposite the sheriff's office. Others were taking cover behind sacks, or in the alleys. The remaining riders flanked the office. Aside from them, the road was clearing rapidly as Clearwater's citizens scurried for cover.

'Hopeman,' Luther shouted, 'sundown is a-coming and it's time to bring Tyler out.'

'No chance,' Hopeman shouted from within the office.

'Then I'll be a-coming.'

At the end of the road, Jim and Armstrong glanced at each other.

'We got to get into a better position,' Armstrong said, 'or we ain't going to help here.'

Jim nodded then pointed down the road and ordered Armstrong to skirt around the back of town and attack Luther from the other end of the road.

Armstrong nodded and edged to the wall. Jim joined him and they backed away from Luther, keeping their guns holstered to appear that they weren't aiming to cause trouble. But, on the edge of town, they parted.

Armstrong ran across the road, then disappeared behind the church, and Jim dashed around the back of the stables and towards the Lucky Star.

He'd reached the back of the saloon when a volley of gunfire blasted out on the road. Jim gritted his teeth and charged down the alley beside the saloon. At the end, he slid to a halt and peered out on to the road, but he'd emerged level with two men who were hunkered down on the board-walk and firing at the office.

Jim darted his head back to avoid their seeing him, and when the next volley of gunfire ended, he ventured another glance.

But the nearest man *had* seen him. He fired three rapid shots that whistled past Jim's nose, forcing him to dart back into the alley.

Jim debated heading back down the alley, but as that'd probably get him a bullet in the back he rocked back on his heels, then charged out on to the boardwalk.

On the run he ripped an arc of gunfire sideways, scything through the nearest man's chest. The man staggered off the edge of the boardwalk, his gun falling from his slack fingers as he clutched his chest then rolled to lie sprawled on the ground.

But the second man swung round and blasted lead at Jim.

In desperation, Jim leapt to the ground, skidding on his shoulder as he hurtled into the road. On the ground, he fired, winging the man's arm and wheeling him away.

Jim took more careful aim, but from the saloon roof a man fired down at him, the bullet pluming into the earth beside Jim's arm. Jim rolled on his back and, with his back braced, fired up. The shot was wild and, with no time to reload, he rolled back to the boardwalk, slugs tearing into the earth behind his tumbling form.

On the boardwalk he rolled to his knees and grabbed the first man's gun.

The wounded man was clawing his way down the boardwalk towards him, his gun thrust out, but Jim ripped lead into his chest, slamming him to the timbers, then collected his gun. He craned his neck out to venture a glance up at the roof, but a warning shot forced him to dart back to the wall.

Out in the road around a dozen riders circled before the sheriff's office, and more men were running in from both sides.

Jim took a deep breath, then, with his guns thrust out, charged into the road. He danced round on the spot and fired up at the man on the roof.

His first shots were wild, but the man clutched his chest and slipped to his knees, then tumbled down the roof. As he crashed to the ground beside Jim, Jim swirled round to see that Armstrong had climbed on to the church roof and, from that vantage point, had shot the man. He acknowledged Jim then swung round and fired down at the men in the road.

In confusion, they scattered and Jim added to their problems by hunkering down on the edge of the boardwalk and blasting two men from their mounts.

Hopeman and Newall, spurred on by this success, flung open the office door and laid down an arc of deadly gunfire that took another two riders.

Luther barked orders and all the men who were on foot fled to their horses, gathering them on the run, and backed them across the road. But before they could regroup the lawmen and Armstrong peppered gunfire at them from different angles and, in panic, they pranced their horses back.

And when the lawmen knocked another man from his horse Luther swung his horse around and galloped out of town, throwing up a huge cloud of dust in his desperation to flee Clearwater. His men trailed after him, only a few having the bravado to holler and rip gunfire into the air.

On the run, Jim fired at a straggler who had failed to mount his horse. But when both his guns clicked on empty chambers he charged after him and grabbed his arm. The man tried to tear himself away, but Jim gained a firmer grip, then pulled him around.

He swung back his fist, ready to slug him to the ground, but then saw the green bandanna around the man's neck, a familiar embroidered pattern covering the corner, and froze.

The man stared back at him, expecting Jim to hit him, but when Jim continued to stare, he shook himself free, then bundled Jim away.

As Jim floundered on the ground, the man dashed to his horse, mounted it, and galloped away. Jim rubbed his face, forcing his shock to recede, then reloaded and fired at the fleeing riders, but by then they were all surging out of town.

Still, he dashed down the road to his horse and mounted it. He tugged his steed around and hurried down the road after Luther's men.

But by the time he passed the sheriff's office Armstrong had climbed down from the church roof. He leapt out into the road to block his way. Jim pulled his horse to a halt, almost unseating himself in the process, then moved to pass him, but Armstrong leapt to the side to block his route again.

'Move!' Jim shouted. 'They're getting away.'

'And let them go, unless you want to die.'

Jim glared down the road at the riders, now several hundred yards beyond the edge of town. Then, with a reluctant slap of a fist against his thigh, he acknowledged the recklessness of his pursuit and dismounted.

As Gene Trentham emerged from his workshop to collect his latest business, Jim crossed the road to the sheriff's office. Armstrong was at his side and looking at him with his brow furrowed, but Jim firmed his jaw instead of explaining himself.

On the boardwalk, Hopeman slapped his back, then moved on to congratulating Armstrong. The sheriff even offered to deputize Armstrong, but Armstrong refused, although he did accept the offer of a coffee.

Inside the office, Jim sat on the edge of his desk as Hopeman paced across the room to stand before the corner cell and peer at Tyler through the bars.

But despite the failure of the rescue attempt, Tyler sat on his bunk, clutching his knees to his chest and smiling.

'Don't gloat, Sheriff,' he muttered. 'Luther *will* succeed.'

'He will not,' Hopeman snapped, then joined Jim, who relayed the details of Max's presumed ransacking of Monty's store in his search for something, then his unsuccessful attempt to ambush him.

Throughout, Hopeman snorted his ill-opinion of Max, but when Jim mentioned his idea about Bart Haley being a potential witness, he brightened, then frowned on hearing of his demise.

'That sure is a pity. If we're going to convict Tyler, we need proof.'

'Bart wanted to tell me something. He thought the fact that he saw nothing was far more interesting than I thought it was.'

Hopeman nodded. 'Perhaps he was right. If the killer didn't leave the pass that way, somebody should have seen him.'

Jim glanced at Armstrong, but bit back mentioning what was obvious to them all. The only man who had come out of Black Pass was Monty Elwood.

'Either way,' Jim murmured, 'now that Luther Wade has made his intentions clear, it ain't going to be easy to get Tyler to trial.'

'You're right.' Hopeman sighed. 'And I guess I now have to admit we need help to sort this out.'

Hopeman located a scrap of paper on his desk and scrawled a quick message on it. He passed the note to Deputy Newell and ordered him to go to the telegraph office in Fall Creek as fast as he could and wire a message to Marshal Kirby.

Newell turned to the door, but Jim shuffled off the side of the desk and volunteered to go instead. And when Newell raised no objection, Jim took the message from him.

'Come now. Got the man who shot Benny Lawson,' Jim said, reading the message. In the doorway, he tipped his hat to Hopeman. 'I guess if we're lucky, Kirby will be here by sundown tomorrow.'

'And,' Hopeman said, 'I reckon we can sure hold out against Luther for that long.'

7

Jim galloped out of Clearwater, but, on the edge of town, he slowed and searched for Luther's trail.

As he'd half-expected, recent tracks headed towards Devil's Canyon, but he wasn't a tracker and, when the canyon appeared on the horizon the trail had already gone cold.

On his own, he didn't dare head into the canyon, so he spent a fruitless hour scouting around the outskirts of his father's land.

But when he failed to refind Luther's tracks, he accepted that he wouldn't be able to both get the message to Marshal Kirby and pick up Luther's trail this evening, so with some reluctance, he headed towards Fall Creek instead.

But as he closed on the trail, he saw that his father was using the last of the day's light to patrol his borders. With his hat raised high he hailed him.

Caleb hailed him back and, despite his need to hurry, Jim stopped.

'You fine now, Father?' he asked when Caleb joined him.

'Yeah.' Caleb considered Jim, then sighed. 'And if you're checking up on me to see whether I'm planning to kill Tyler, you don't need to. I got no desire to see him until he's swinging on the end of a rope.'

'Glad to hear it. But I ain't checking on you. I'm heading to Fall Creek to get a message to Marshal Kirby.'

'To me, you were just roaming around, trying to decide whether or not to see me.' Caleb flashed a grim smile. 'And no matter how bad things are between us, I can't believe you need to do that.'

'I *was* roaming around, but I was trying to pick up the tracks of those outlaws who tried to free Tyler.'

'Free him?' Caleb gasped, his eyes flaring.

'Yeah. Luther Wade roared into town

92

and fair shot up the place, but we saw him off.'

'Then you did well.' Caleb glanced back into the hills then along the trail. 'But you were looking in the wrong place. Aside from you, nobody's passed by me all day.'

'Obliged for the information.' Jim turned to the trail, but Caleb raised a hand and he turned back.

'Are you worried this Luther might try to seize Tyler again?'

'If I don't get help from Marshal Kirby, he might.'

Caleb nodded, then hunched his shoulders and, for just a moment, his eyes flashed with a hint of warmth. And when he spoke, his carefree voice suggested the considerate man who had enlightened Jim's childhood years.

'Son, let me pass that message on for you, and you can carry on searching for him.' Caleb smiled, but when Jim returned a shake of the head, he removed his hat and clutched it before him. 'It'll be my way of apologizing for nearly shooting Tyler. And for just accusing you. And for everything I've . . . everything.'

Unable to face encouraging a discussion that he didn't think he'd ever have, but to which he now didn't have the time to devote, Jim glanced at the hills. He ran his gaze over the many places in which Luther's gang could have holed up, then at the large and red sun on the western horizon.

He nodded, then passed Caleb the note Hopeman had given him.

'And maybe once this is over we can . . . ' Jim coughed to clear his throat, finding that he couldn't even ask whether he could visit the family home for the first time since his mother had died.

'Maybe.' Caleb pocketed the note and, without further word, swung his horse round to head towards Fall Creek, leaving Jim to watch his back recede into the distance, then turn to the hills.

Jim took his father's advice and

resumed his search out of sight of his father's land, but, as the sun dipped below the horizon and the light-level plummeted, he still couldn't find Luther's tracks. So he decided to use the weak rays of the low crescent moon to risk scouting into the first length of the canyon.

But he did resolve to stay within a few minutes' riding of the entrance.

The barren gash that was the canyon was twenty miles long and consisted of one long arc with only the most withered of vegetation flanking its rocky sides.

On either side of the trail, a tangle of caves, boulders and weathered rock formation spread out. So, when Jim reached the canyon, he hunched forward in the saddle and glanced at each passing cave and source of a likely ambush while maintaining a brisk pace.

He found no obvious signs that Luther had headed here, so within fifteen minutes, he turned to leave, but as he reached the exit, he saw a lone

95

rider standing on the trail, facing him.

Jim peered into the gloom, then smiled to himself and hailed the rider.

'What you doing here, Armstrong?' he said.

'Hopeman ordered me to scout around while you sent that message.' Armstrong considered Jim, his eyebrows raised with a silent question. But when Jim just drew alongside, he pointed at the ground. 'And I reckon we're both interested in these.'

Jim peered at the messed-up ground, seeing nothing but the usual prints on the trail, their forms almost lost in the shadows.

'What am I looking at?'

'The prints made by a group of riders as they hurried into the canyon.' Armstrong looked up at Jim and smiled. 'And I reckon they'll be Luther's tracks.'

Jim kept his jaw firm. 'What makes you think I'm looking for him?'

'Because I reckon you got someone else to deliver that message, and searching for Luther's gang is the only thing I can think of that you could be doing. Trouble is, I don't know why you're doing it — unless you got yourself a death wish.'

Jim considered Armstrong, but then shrugged.

'You're right about what I'm doing, but I got no intention of explaining myself.'

'I thought as much.' Armstrong peered ahead into the darkening interior of Devil's Canyon, then turned back to Jim. 'Still, you want some help in finding him?'

★   ★   ★

Luther's encampment was in a narrow gully and set back from the main trail through the canyon. His gang had slipped under an overhang that hid them from view from all directions but head on.

Their camp-fire was low and guarded and just strong enough to drive away the night chill. Their horses were tethered in the deepest part of the overhang.

In the thirty minutes that Armstrong and Jim had watched them from the edge of the slope opposite they had showed no inclination to take their horses to the dribbling stream that ran through the pass.

Now, with the full onset of night, the men bustled around the camp-fire, passing plates around.

With the men now confident in their security, their voices grew louder and boisterous. And when they'd eaten, they nominated Woodward — Jim learnt his name from the taunts they directed at him — to water their horses on the basis that he had been the last one to leave Clearwater earlier.

On his own, Woodward led the horses down to the stream.

As he passed their position, Jim leaned over the edge of the slope to peer down. With his eyes narrowed, he confirmed that he *was* the man with the green bandanna.

Armstrong watched Jim and when he shuffled back, he leaned towards him.

'Are we going to ambush them?' he asked. 'Or are we just going to watch them?'

'You're going to watch them. I'm going to ambush this one.'

Before Armstrong could question his orders, Jim patted Armstrong's shoulder, then slipped back from the edge.

Bent double he edged from his position and down the slope, keeping about thirty yards back from Woodward and staying in the deep shadows between the boulders that flanked the gully.

When he emerged by the stream, Woodward was around thirty yards to his right, his gaze locked on the horses.

Jim watched him, confirming that he wasn't being particularly observant, then slipped around the edge of a thick tangle of thickets until he was ten yards back from him.

Then he stood tall and drew his

Peacemaker, not risking alerting him by trying to get closer.

'Reach,' he ordered.

Woodward flinched and swirled at the hip, his hand whirling to his gun, but on seeing the gun aimed at his chest he raised his hand.

'What you want with me?' he grunted, then narrowed his eyes to peer into the gloom. 'Deputy.'

'I got a question to ask you.'

Woodward paced round on the spot to face Jim, then spread his hands.

'Ask away,' he said, raising his voice.

Jim glanced up the slope towards the campsite, but judged that unless Woodward shouted he was unlikely to attract anyone's attention. He ordered Woodward to drop his gunbelt, then pointed at the bandanna around his neck.

'Where you get that?'

Woodward raised a hand to finger the bandanna, displaying the embroidered letter Z in the corner, then shrugged.

'Had it a long time.'

'You not get it from a woman?'

Woodward blinked, and when he spoke his voice was lower and less assured than before.

'Don't know about no woman.'

'She lived in Clearwater five years ago when Tyler Coleman was here, but then she disappeared.'

'I got no idea what you — '

'You *do* know something.' Jim firmed his gun hand. 'And you'll tell me why you're wearing the bandanna I gave Zelma Hayden.'

Woodward shuffled from foot to foot, but his gaze flicked over Jim's right shoulder.

Jim stood tall, listening, but then, on hearing a crunch as of a foot grinding into loose dirt, he turned at the hip and arced his Peacemaker round. But when he was fully turned it was to face Luther, his other men spread out around him with their guns aimed at him.

And in their midst was Armstrong with two men holding him from behind with his arms thrust up his back.

To Luther's grunted command, Jim threw his gun on the ground, but he still stood with his posture casual and ready to make a stand if the chance presented itself.

'What you doing with Woodward?' Luther asked, packing forward from the group to stand before Jim.

'I'm asking him a question.'

Luther flicked his gaze at Woodward.

'He don't look like he wants to answer.'

'He'll answer either here or in jail, but I will get an answer.' Luther snorted and glanced back at the phalanx of men behind him, then turned and folded his arms.

'About what?'

'It's the woman,' Woodward said. 'He's asking about the woman.'

Armstrong grunted and tried to wrestle himself free of the men holding him, but they gripped his arms more tightly. Still he struggled and, with a huge lunge of his right arm, hurled one of the men from him.

Using the distraction, Jim dropped to one knee, his questing hand lunging for his gun, but a warning shot from Luther plumed into the ground, inches from his fingers, and forced him to raise his hand and stand.

With at least ten men training their guns on him, he could only watch Armstrong's attempted escape.

Armstrong scrambled himself free of the other man holding him, but by then Luther was at his side. And at the moment Armstrong gained his freedom, Luther swung his gun back-handed, clipping Armstrong's temple. The blow landed with a dull thud, spinning Armstrong away and, in an instant, he slumped to the ground.

Luther glared down at him and tapped a foot against his chest, but when Armstrong didn't even return a grunt, he swirled round to face Woodward.

'Now,' he said, 'how did he learn about the woman?'

Woodward slipped the bandanna

from his neck and waved it at Luther.

'He recognized this.'

'He did, did he? Now, that's mighty interesting.' Luther stalked past Woodward to Jim's side.

'And I want an answer from one of you,' Jim muttered, then jutted his jaw and glared at Luther. 'Why do you have it?'

'I'll answer.' Luther licked his thin lips. 'But are you man enough to hear the answer?'

'I am. Just tell me what happened to Zelma. I'll listen to your side of what happened, but whatever the truth, I have to know.'

Luther rubbed his chin with the barrel of his gun, then chuckled.

'You got some kind of feelings for her?'

'I did. But that was many years ago. Now I just want to know what you did with her.' Jim gulped. 'Whatever that may be.'

Luther holstered his gun, then backed away from Jim. He paraded before him, throwing out his legs with exaggerated movements. On the fifth pass, he swung to a halt, then glanced down at Armstrong, then at Woodward, then at the other men before turning his gaze back on Jim. He smiled.

'That truth will cost.'

'What cost?'

Luther laughed. 'You know.'

'I don't. Just tell me!'

'As you need me to spell it out,' Luther said then glanced around his arc of men, delivering a low chuckle, 'I'll tell you what happened to Zelma Hayden when Tyler Coleman goes free.'

'Tyler ain't going free.'

'Then you'll remain ignorant.' Luther paced back and forth before Jim twice more, but then swung to a halt and cocked his head to the side as he peered into Jim's eyes. 'And you'll die in ignorance on this very spot.'

'Why you — ' Jim raised a fist and advanced on Luther, but Woodward grabbed his arm from behind and held him back. Jim stood with his arm raised, then rolled his shoulders and threw Woodward away from him to stand free. 'You won't get away with this.'

'I will.' Luther pointed a firm finger at Jim. 'And if you want to hear the truth about Zelma, you will deliver Tyler to me.'

'I'll never do an outlaw's bidding.'

Luther drew his gun and sighted Jim's forehead.

'Then this is your last chance, Deputy. Give me Tyler, or die.'

8

'I'm a lawman,' Jim muttered. 'There ain't no way I'm breaking the law for you.'

Luther tightened his trigger finger. His eyes widened.

'Then you'll — '

A gunshot ripped out. Despite his determined stance, Jim flinched, but then staggered back a pace when he saw the gun wheel from Luther's hand.

Luther snapped his head round to search for who had shot at him, then dived for his gun, but a second shot blasted it away from his questing fingers. He barked out an order and his men dropped to their haunches. They took up defence positions, then blasted in all directions, firing blindly into the darkness.

But one man spun back as a high slug ripped into his neck and a second man toppled forward as lead scythed into his guts.

Luther urged everyone to fall back. He lunged for Jim, but Jim took advantage of everyone's confusion and batted Luther's hand away, then slugged his jaw, the blow wheeling him to the ground. With his head down, he charged for Luther's gun.

He dived, rolling over the gun and dragging it into his grasp, then continued the roll until he came up on his feet and running for the men guarding Armstrong. Both these men were trying to drag their prisoner into the lee of a giant boulder, but Jim ripped lead into the first man, slamming him back against the boulder.

And a second shot from his hidden rescuer cut the second man's legs from under him.

Then sustained gunfire erupted all around Jim, but it was all wild firing from the outlaws and aimed in no particular direction. He slid to a halt beside Armstrong and grabbed his arm.

Armstrong looked up with his eyes rolling, but Jim slapped his face and peered down into his eyes.

'We got one chance to escape,' he muttered. 'Either move or die.'

Armstrong provided a determined nod, then pushed himself to his feet. He stood stooped and swaying, but then swung round and, with Jim thrusting a hand under his arm, they shuffled into the darkness.

Luther barked out orders to recapture them, but Jim staggered into the thickets seeking the darkest shadows. Within seconds of brushing past the first tangle of coarse wood, footsteps pounded after him. Lead whistled past his shoulder and he swirled round to see a man charging after him.

Jim turned at the hip and blasted this man in the chest, the man so close he ran on for a few paces before barging into him. Jim shrugged him off and stood for a moment, waiting for the next attacker, but when nobody followed him, he turned.

With Armstrong growing in strength with every pace, they staggered ever further into the darkness, heading for the densest patch of thickets they could find.

Luther continued to shout orders, but they grew fainter and he was getting no discipline from men who were pinned down by determined gunfire.

'You reckon that's Hopeman out there?' Armstrong asked when they paused for breath.

'Could be.' Jim released his hold of Armstrong's arm and let him sit, then hunkered down in a guarding position. 'But we need to be quiet.'

'And grateful,' Armstrong whispered.

★ ★ ★

It was well into the night when Jim and Armstrong returned to Clearwater. Their rescuer's gunfire had forced Luther to scurry back to his camp, and they had taken that opportunity to return to their horses and leave Devil's Canyon.

They found no hint as to who had rescued them, not that they stayed long enough to search for any clues, and when they returned to Clearwater Hopeman didn't mention the incident. As Jim didn't want to mention why he'd got them into such a dangerous situation, he said nothing beyond confirming that the message to Marshal Kirby had been wired.

While he'd been away Deputy Newell had searched Max Malloy's house and found nearly $1,000 in small bills. This suggested that Max had been involved with Tyler in the robbery that led to Benny's death five years ago, but like everything else Jim had learned recently, that raised more questions than it provided answers.

That night, Hopeman left Jim and Newell on duty while he rode out of town to sleep in a secure spot just off the eastward trail. Armstrong covered the westward trail. With the main routes into Clearwater guarded, Hopeman reckoned the chances of Luther arriving unexpectedly were low.

But even so, Newell and Jim alternated between guarding and sleeping.

With Newell taking the first opportunity to sleep, Jim paced around the office, his thoughts whirling with the discovery that Luther's outlaws knew something about Zelma Hayden's disappearance.

But when Tyler's gaze burned into his neck, he stood before the cell and, for the first time, peered at the prisoner through the bars.

'I hope you ain't getting too settled,' he said. 'Marshal Kirby will be taking you to trial before long and then . . . ' Jim slipped a finger beneath his collar then raised his chin, displaying his neck to Tyler, and gulped.

'And we both know I won't swing.' Tyler sneered. 'You have no proof, and either way, Luther Wade will get me out of here before long.'

'He won't. Your friend had more than twenty men, but we ran him off, no trouble, no trouble at all.'

'That was just a testing sortie.' Tyler glared at Jim through the bars, his eyes bright. 'Save yourself the trouble. Let me go now.'

Jim searched Tyler's arrogant gaze, wondering whether he should question him, and so perhaps learn something that would help his investigation, or perhaps even offer clues as to what had happened to Zelma. But as he didn't want to give the man who had shot his brother and destroyed his family an opportunity to gloat, he turned and headed to his desk.

Behind him, Tyler chuckled then rolled on to his bunk. But Jim still sat and contented himself with listening to the bustle in the road diminish as the evening wore on.

Around midnight Jim woke Newell. While Newell guarded the door Jim carried out the night's first patrol. He strode in a square outside, heading to

113

the four corners where stood the store, the bank, the stables and the saloon.

When he returned he reported the absence of people out on the road. Then, as Newell locked the door, he sat at his desk. He pulled his hat over his face, rocked his feet on to his desk, and shuffled down in his chair.

His problems still reverberated in his mind, but the day had been long and tiring and within minutes lethargy crept into his limbs. But just as the first hints of sleep were dragging him under, a creak sounded nearby.

Jim raised his hat and glanced at Newell, who was already standing by the door, his ear cocked high.

Then it came again — a creak, as of someone creeping across the roof.

Purely using their eyes, Jim and Newell debated whether they should investigate. They decided that Newell should, and the deputy slipped outside, after which Jim edged the door closed behind him and stood by it.

For long moments Jim waited for

Newell to return, but when five minutes had passed he tiptoed into the doorway and hissed an urgent and low request outside.

Again he waited, but the night was as silent as it had been when he had patrolled and the creak from above didn't return. So he glanced outside and hissed another request to Newell.

Still no response came, so this time he paced out on to the boardwalk, his Peacemaker raised and pressed flat to his cheek, his ears straining for the slightest noise.

Then a creak sounded behind him and Jim swirled round, his gun arcing towards whoever had produced the noise. But a heavy weight thudded into the side of his head and he plummeted to his knees.

Heavy footfalls pounded by him, but his vision was blurred and darkness dragged him down.

Darts of light and disorientating visions of the boardwalk outside the office swam around Jim, but when he eventually clawed his way back to consciousness he was sure that he had only been unconscious for a few minutes.

He sat up, rubbing the side of his head, feeling a hard lump above his ear, but guessing that his sudden movement had stopped the man from clubbing him across the temple and possibly knocking him out for longer.

Further down the boardwalk lay Newell, his top half on the boardwalk, his feet in the road.

Jim crawled towards him, but from the corner of his eye he saw the open office door and he slowed to a halt.

He stood, swayed, then staggered to the office. With a shaking hand, he held on to the doorframe and peered inside.

Then, with his Peacemaker thrust out before him, he swung into the office and ran his gaze across the deserted office until it ended at the corner cell.

But the cell door was open and swinging.

And Tyler Coleman had gone.

9

Jim lowered his head, taking deep breaths to regain his composure, then dashed outside and peered up and down the road. But the road was still and he could see no sign of where the kidnapper had taken Tyler.

Still groggy, he hunkered down beside the comatose Newell and slapped his face. He couldn't rouse him, so he dashed to his horse.

He raised a foot to mount his steed, but then lowered it. He had intended to hurry out of town and alert Sheriff Hopeman, but for a reason he couldn't fathom, he was reluctant to do that.

Jim reckoned he had only been unconscious for a few minutes, yet the kidnapper had melted into nowhere.

Sneaking into town quietly and freeing Tyler didn't seem like Luther's tactics. And knocking out himself and

Newell didn't seem the sort of activity Luther would do either. Riding into town, hollering his arrival and firing in all directions seemed to be Luther's approach.

And that suggested the kidnapper wasn't following Luther's orders. And that maybe he hadn't left town either.

So Jim paced out into the road, searching for likely hiding-places.

Then he saw Monty's store. And the door was open. That wasn't unusual — after Max had ransacked the place there was nothing to steal and Armstrong had been using it as his base.

But when he'd completed his patrol earlier the door had been closed. So he strode across the road to the store.

On the boardwalk, he raised his Peacemaker and entered the store.

His eyes were already accustomed to the gloom and within moments his roving gaze picked out the hunched form in the far corner of the store. He narrowed his eyes as he walked towards it and, after two more paces, resolved the form as being the bound and gagged Tyler.

From the corner, Tyler peered back at him, his eyes small embers in the dark.

With his Peacemaker held beside his cheek, Jim crossed the room, walking sideways until he reached Tyler.

But, as he reached out to remove Tyler's gag, a firm footfall sounded behind him.

'Stop right there,' a voice said from behind him.

Jim flinched, but on recognizing Armstrong's voice, he withdrew his hand and stood tall.

'It's me, Jim.'

'I know,' Armstrong said, his tone harsh. 'But if you don't leave Tyler you'll make me do something I don't want to do.'

Jim paced round on the spot to confront Armstrong, who stood before the door, the light from outside framing his bulky form. He glanced at Armstrong's gun, held low with the barrel aimed at his guts and glinting in a stray beam of light, but he kept his hands high and his voice light.

'We both know you won't hurt me.'

Armstrong glanced at his gun, then, with a shrug, holstered it.

'You're right. But damn it, Jim, I'm just doing what you've considered doing for the last few hours. So, just walk away and let me help you.'

Jim cocked his head to the side. 'I can't do that.'

'You can't, but you want to.'

'I don't want to, not even for a moment. I'm a lawman, and I won't break the law to . . . to get information.'

Armstrong tipped back his hat and set his hands on his hips.

'But you disobeyed Sheriff Hopeman's orders to follow Luther Wade.'

'That was the limit of my rule breaking. So, stand aside and let me return Tyler to his cell.'

Armstrong sighed, then beckoned for Jim to join him. Jim stared back for a moment, but then followed Armstrong out on to the boardwalk.

'You need to know about Zelma Hayden,' Armstrong whispered, 'so does it matter what happens to Tyler?'

'I'm desperate to know about her, but I can't release the man who I reckon killed my brother.'

'But you know he's guilty.'

'I don't know that for sure. Only the court can decide. And releasing Tyler sure won't provide justice for my family.'

Armstrong snorted and leaned forwards to appraise Jim, and when Jim just stared back at him, he shook his head.

'I thought you knew.' Armstrong frowned as he fingered his beard. 'Luther doesn't want you to free Tyler because he's his friend. He wants you to release him so that he can kill him.'

Jim narrowed his eyes. 'How do you figure that out?'

'Because Tyler wouldn't ride into Clearwater and almost certain arrest unless he had a mighty good reason.

But as he reckons the court will clear him, you're protecting him while Luther gets himself so riled he'll get himself killed.'

Jim shook his head. 'Whether I believe that or not, I can't release a man who is in my custody.'

Jim moved to return to the store, but Armstrong grabbed his arm, halting him.

'You know Judge Plummer will find Tyler innocent. And that'll destroy your father. Letting Luther kill Tyler will at least give him a chance to move on.'

'I'm a lawman. I won't decide a man's guilt.'

'But Tyler ain't worth what you're risking.'

'He ain't.' Jim shrugged away from Armstrong and turned to the door. 'But I'll find a way to get justice for my brother and discover what happened to Zelma without doing Luther's bidding.'

★   ★   ★

Jim locked Tyler up, then dragged Deputy Newell into the office and roused him.

When Newell was sufficiently alert, Jim told him what he hoped would be a plausible version of events: he had come out of the office, found Newell unconscious, searched, then found a lone, would-be kidnapper attempting to leave town with Tyler. He had wrested Tyler from him but the man had escaped.

Jim glared at Tyler's cell when he'd finished his explanation, but Tyler didn't contradict him.

Newell then headed out of town to report what had happened to Hopeman, who returned to hear the report first hand.

Jim hated lying but he ran through his story, keeping the details — and the lies — to a minimum.

As Hopeman believed the tale and saw no reason to change their tactics, they returned to their previous routine of Hopeman and Armstrong guarding the routes into Clearwater and Jim and Newell taking turns to sleep.

The rest of the night passed without incident and, at sun-up, Hopeman and Armstrong returned to the office.

With nobody in the mood for conversation, the four men set in for a quiet day of waiting for Marshal Kirby.

An hour into the day, a messenger arrived and reported that Marshal Kirby and a group of deputies had boarded the train in Green Valley and they would be in Fall Creek by early afternoon.

With this good news the lawmen tucked into breakfast, their mood lightening.

But two hours later another messenger arrived to report that a dozen or more rough types had descended on the telegraph station in Fall Creek. Despite the efforts of the office to confuse them, they'd discovered the message that Marshal Kirby was on his way.

Then they'd left, heading west along the train tracks towards the approaching train.

Hopeman pressed for more details, but although the messenger was only passing on the information second hand, everything pointed to this gang being Luther Wade's men.

'Marshal Kirby will see them off,' Hopeman said. 'I've never met that lawman, but everyone says he's formidable.'

'Even Kirby could struggle against that many men,' Jim said. 'But I could intercept the train and escort him on a safe route here.'

Hopeman rubbed his chin as he considered, then nodded.

'I'll go with him,' Armstrong said, jumping to his feet.

Jim opened his mouth to complain, but when Hopeman stared at him with a firm-jawed expression that said he supported Armstrong's offer, he nodded and turned to the door.

With Armstrong beside him they left

the office and without debate rode out of town.

Fall Creek was three hours away and on the way neither man discussed what had happened last night. Although, from Armstrong's clenched jaw, Jim gathered what he thought of his refusal to let him release Tyler.

But both men being lost in their own thoughts, they didn't waste time and arrived at a water-tower fifty miles down the tracks from Fall Creek in good time.

With a few terse comments they agreed to wait for the train here.

For twenty minutes they stood on either side of the tracks. Jim looked west towards the oncoming train and Armstrong looked east in case Luther was still heading down the tracks.

But now the silence preyed on Jim's thoughts and he backed down the track to stand beside Armstrong.

'Guess I'm obliged to you for volunteering for this,' he said.

'Somebody had to stop you getting

yourself killed,' Armstrong said, his jaw set firm and his gaze still set east. 'But I don't understand why you wanted to come here. I'm sure that marshal can take care of himself.'

'Every source of information has turned up blank, and I reckon Luther Wade is my last chance of getting proof that Tyler killed my brother.' Jim sighed. 'But if I get the chance to capture him, can I trust you?'

'You can,' Armstrong muttered, his tone hurt. 'I'd do nothing to endanger the life of a lawman.'

Jim nodded. 'But you would try to free the man who killed my brother.'

'I told you my reasoning. I was just helping you by doing something you couldn't do yourself.' Armstrong turned to look at Jim, his gaze cold. 'And you can trust me.'

Jim nodded.

'Then I will,' he said, and made to head back down the track.

'But you never explained your full reasoning,' Armstrong snapped, his harsh tone halting Jim. 'And I'd like to know whether I can trust you when the bullets start flying.'

'I guess I deserve that.' Jim stared down the tracks, then sighed. 'But I can't say it clearer than the fact that I'm a lawman. I have to do the right thing.'

'Even if that means never knowing what happened to a woman you once loved?'

'Yeah. Knowing her fate won't bring her back.'

'She doesn't have to be dead. You could be risking her life by not letting Luther have Tyler.'

This comment dragged a rumble from Jim's guts. From the moment he'd seen the bandanna he'd assumed the outlaws had killed Zelma.

'Even that,' Jim murmured. Then he raised his jaw and firmed his voice. 'Yeah, even that. It ain't my place to make the rules. I just — '

'Don't lecture me on what is right and what is wrong. I just know that no law is in the right if it might hurt an innocent woman just because of a worthless man like Tyler Coleman.'

Jim flared his eyes. 'Then I can't explain my reasoning to you.'

Jim bunched the reins and with a determined swing of his arms he turned his horse and headed down the track.

'You can't,' Armstrong shouted after him, 'but answer me this — if you're so sure of your actions, why didn't you tell Sheriff Hopeman about Zelma? And why didn't you tell him what I tried to do last night?'

Jim slowed his horse to a halt, then turned to look at Armstrong. But from the corner of his eye, he saw the train appear ahead, its shimmering form emerging from out of the low heat haze.

'The train's a-coming,' he said.

Armstrong uttered a low snort then nudged his horse forwards to join Jim.

'Are you avoiding answering because you don't know, or because you dare not admit the answer to yourself.'

'Does it matter?'

'Yeah, because I might get another

chance to resolve your problem, and knowing what you really want will help me decide what I should do.'

'Then remember this,' Jim said, waggling a firm finger at Armstrong. 'I won't break the law and I won't let you break the law either.'

Armstrong glanced away to watch the approaching train.

'Then I understand you.'

Jim nodded. 'But what about you? Because I still don't understand why you risked your own life with that misguided plan to help me.'

Armstrong nodded ahead. 'The train's a-coming.'

Jim continued to glare at Armstrong, but when no further answers were forthcoming, he turned to face the train.

10

When the train arrived Jim and Armstrong boarded it while the engineers took on water. From the engineers' brisk attitude and the passengers' calm demeanour, Jim reckoned they hadn't seen Luther Wade.

So, after securing their horses in the end carriage, they paced down through the carriages, searching for Marshal Kirby.

'Any idea what this marshal looks like?' Armstrong asked when they reached the last carriage.

'Nope, but his sort are usually obvious.' Jim smiled and nodded towards the end of the carriage. 'And I reckon that's our man.'

A group of men had commandeered the end of the carriage. They sprawled over the seats, gazing at the other passengers, and their surly silence had forced the middle of the carriage to remain unoccupied.

In their midst sat a man in a black coat, his grey-flecked and trim moustache nestling beneath an aquiline nose and flint eyes. And although he kept his gaze through the window, Jim reckoned it was his reflection that he was watching.

Jim took the lead in filing down the aisle. As he entered the unoccupied part of the carriage the men swung round to stare up at him.

One man thrust out a leg across the aisle, blocking Jim's route.

Jim stopped, looked down at the leg, then rolled his gaze to the owner of the leg, who also glared up at him, a surly grin on his face.

'Where you going?' the man asked.

'I'm here to meet the marshal,' Jim said. He put on a huge and false smile. 'And I'd be obliged if you'd let us join you.'

The man's gaze didn't flicker with even a moment's surprise.

'Join us?' The man snorted. 'Got no use for no new deputies.'

Outside, the conductor's hollering rippled down the carriage and with a lurch the train started off for Fall Creek.

Jim rested a hand on a seat to keep his balance.

'We don't want to be deputy marshals. I'm Sheriff Hopeman's deputy.' Jim gestured over his shoulder. 'And this here is — '

'You didn't listen. We got no need for *anyone* joining us.'

'I'd prefer to hear that from the marshal.'

As the man sneered, Jim turned and peered down the aisle at the man he presumed was Marshal Kirby.

For long moments he stared at him, then Kirby swung his cold gaze from the window to look up at Jim.

'Why are you still here?' he murmured, his voice low and uninterested.

'Because I'm escorting you to Clearwater.'

Kirby feigned a yawn. 'I know the way.'

'I'm sure you do, but you don't know that Luther Wade's gang intercepted your message saying you were coming. They'll be lying in wait somewhere between here and Clearwater.'

'And?'

'And I know plenty of hidden trails. And I reckon we should get off the train before Fall Creek and use them.'

'Do you?' Kirby snorted, his comment dragging a barked laugh from the other men. 'I don't need no deputy sheriff from some no-hope town like Clearwater ordering me around.'

'That ain't an order. It was a suggestion.'

Kirby glanced around the deputies with his eyebrows raised, his exasperated gaze gathering laughs as it travelled across his men.

'Then I'll tell you what you can do with your suggestion.' Kirby leaned forward, then offered Jim a physically impossible set of activities he could do to himself on his way back to Clearwater.

Throughout, Jim remained stone-faced and when the tirade ended, he raised his eyebrows.

'If I tried to do that, my saddle would get in the way, but either way, the suggestion is sound.'

Kirby snorted and turned to stare out the window.

'And either way, stay out of my way.'

'We ain't.' Jim glanced over his shoulder at the nearest unoccupied seat. 'We're with you all the way to Clearwater and, if necessary, all the way back to Green Valley.'

Kirby sneered then muttered another taunt, but Jim didn't stay to hear it and headed to his seat.

Armstrong lingered for a moment, staring at the sprawl of impassive deputies, then sat beside Jim. As the train built up to its full speed, he leaned to Jim.

'He can't treat you like that,' he whispered.

Jim shrugged. 'Kirby is no different from most US marshals I've met. They're all as arrogant as they come, until you prove your worth.'

'And you reckon before we reach Clearwater we'll get the chance to prove our worth?'

Jim nodded, then folded his arms and leaned back in his seat.

He stared through the window, watching the landscape pass as he searched for any sign that Luther was attempting to raid the train.

But for the next hour the train trundled along without incident.

Fifteen miles out of Fall Creek the train pulled into Lockwood, the last stop before their destination.

Jim craned his neck to glance along the platform, but the only people waiting for the train were two elderly women. He looked over his shoulder, but Marshal Kirby was leaning back in his chair with his hat pulled over his eyes, and his deputies were maintaining their studied bored attitude.

'They just don't seem interested,' Armstrong said, joining Jim in considering the lawmen.

'And that's what they want everyone to think,' Jim said. 'But one of them will have already checked who got on board.'

Within two minutes, the train lurched to a start.

Jim was just settling down into his seat again when two men dashed from the station house and headed for the train. They chased along the platform to gain the same speed as the train. Then, with a helping hand from the conductor, they leapt on board as the train trundled out of the station.

Jim patted Armstrong's shoulder, but Armstrong was already leaning to the side to watch these men disappear from view.

'The first man was Woodward,' he murmured. 'The other man was Jameson, one of the men who jumped me in Devil's Canyon.'

Jim patted his holster. 'Then an

ambush is imminent.'

Armstrong swung from his seat and moved to head down the carriage towards Kirby, but Jim grabbed his arm and pulled him back. With a single raised eyebrow, he conveyed that this was their chance to prove their worth.

Armstrong rocked back and forth on his heels, but then nodded. With that agreement they headed down the carriage.

The gazes of Kirby's deputies bored into Jim's back, but he kept his head set forward and left the carriage. One at a time, he and Armstrong jumped over the gap to the second carriage and headed inside.

With Jim leading they paced down the carriage, both men looking at each of the passengers as they searched for Woodward and Jameson, but they reached the end without seeing them.

'They got on to this carriage, didn't they?' Armstrong asked.

'Yeah, I'm sure — '

The carriage door swung open to

reveal Woodward standing in the doorway. But he saw Jim, flinched, then slammed the door shut.

Jim broke into a run and reached the door a few seconds after it closed. He stood by the wall as he waited for Armstrong to join him, then threw open the door. He ventured a glance outside, but saw nobody, then dashed through the doorway and headed for the door to the next carriage.

But when he opened that door, he didn't see Woodward.

Both men stared down the carriage aisle, then both their gazes rose to the train roof. They exchanged a nod.

Jim climbed up the ladder on the side of the carriage. He glanced on to the roof, but a gunshot scythed past his ear and into the carriage wall behind him, forcing him to duck.

He counted to ten, then glanced up, but it was to see Woodward and Jameson shuffling down the carriage roof and away from him. Keeping his body pressed flat to the side of the train, Jim snaked up the last two steps and rolled on to the roof. He lay flat and waited for Armstrong to join him.

Then the two men edged down the roof after Woodward and Jameson. But they stayed doubled over with their hands held out to help them maintain a steady path despite the swaying of the train.

Woodward glanced over his shoulder, then grunted and attracted Jameson's attention. The two men swirled round and hunkered down. They blasted a single shot apiece at them, but the train was swaying so much the shots were wild.

Even so, Jim and Armstrong hurled themselves flat and, with their elbows braced against the train roof, they took careful aim at the two men.

In return, Woodward and Jameson ripped out four shots at them. Two slugs whistled over their heads and two cannoned into the roof before them. But Jim and Armstrong attuned themselves to the rhythm of the train, then fired. Jim's shot was wild, but Armstrong's tore into Jameson's shoulder, spinning him round and to his knees.

Woodward fired again, then swung round and grabbed Jameson's unhurt arm. He checked on him. Then, with Woodward holding Jameson up, the two men lumbered down the carriage away from them and, after a short run, vaulted the gap to the next carriage and headed on.

Jim fired another speculative shot, then jumped to his feet. With Armstrong as his side, they hurtled down the carriage roof.

They reached the gap and vaulted it, then charged after the fleeing men, gaining on them with every pace. Woodward glanced back and flinched, possibly in surprise at seeing how close they were.

He fired over his shoulder, the bullet scything past Jim's arm and, as Woodward took more careful aim, Jim threw himself down to slide across the train roof and plough into Woodward's legs.

Woodward tumbled over Jim's sliding form. But Jim was the first to right himself. He swung round and, on his back, fired sideways at Woodward. From close range, the shot tore into Woodward's guts.

A pained screech escaped Woodward's lips. He staggered towards Jim on his knees, his hands clutching at his belly. With his eyes rolling, he fell on him, his body pressing Jim's gun hand into the roof.

With Woodward's dead weight lying on him, Jim looked up to see that Armstrong and Jameson were now slugging it out. Jameson was injured but he kept his bloodied shoulder away from Armstrong and led with his right fist.

But after delivering two wild round-armed blows that whistled short of Armstrong's head, Armstrong danced in with both his hands clutched together, aiming to hammer Jameson

142

from the train roof. But with surprising grace, Jameson ducked the blow and, as Armstrong teetered, off-balance, he kicked Armstrong's legs from under him.

Armstrong landed heavily on his back and, as he floundered, Jameson scrambled for his gun and aimed it down at Armstrong's chest. But five feet to his side, Jim squeezed his arm out from beneath Woodward and ripped a low shot into Jameson's hip.

Jameson staggered a pace, his gun falling from his slackening fingers, but a second shot to the back wheeled him from the train roof.

As Armstrong nodded his thanks, Jim grabbed Woodward's arm to tug him away, but as Woodward's head rose, bright eyes peered at him and, with a short head-butt, Woodward slammed his forehead into Jim's nose. The blow came from close to and was weak, but it surprised Jim and snapped his head back to slam into the train roof.

He shook himself and, through

blurred vision, looked up to see Woodward swing his gun round to fire at him. Jim swung his own gun up, but a shot rang out.

Jim gritted his teeth, but Woodward rocked back on his haunches, then tumbled away, gunsmoke rising from a hole in his back.

But as he fell his clawed lunge grabbed Jim's jacket and his weight dragged Jim with him. The two men rolled to the side of the roof. In desperation, Jim dug his elbows in, but he couldn't get enough traction and slid to the edge of the roof.

Then Woodward plummeted over the side, his body disappearing from sight, but in a moment, Jim was following him, Woodward's death grip dragging him down. At speed, he slid over the edge, but he heard a scrambling from behind and Armstrong's hands clutched his waist, stopping his flight with a jarring shudder.

When he'd blinked away his shock, it was to find that Woodward had a firm grip of his arm and was dangling below him. Jim was bent over the edge at the waist, but Armstrong was holding him. Woodward glared up at him.

'Seems we'll both die,' he said with mocking laughter in his voice.

'Nobody has to die.'

Woodward threw up his left arm and grabbed Jim's right arm, grunting with the effort. The extra grip dragged Jim another few inches forward.

'You'll regret shooting me.' Woodward chuckled. 'It'll be a painful end for you lying by the track with a whole lot of broken bones.'

'Even with those bullets in you, you could still live. Quit struggling and I'll get you to a doctor.'

'And then?'

'Depends on what you've done.' Jim glanced down at the ground speeding past below him. 'And especially about what you did with Zelma.'

'I'm telling you nothing about . . . ' Woodward grimaced, his eyes glazing as his grip weakened. He slid down Jim's arm. 'I'm . . . I'm . . . '

His hand opened and he slipped from Jim, but Jim lunged and grabbed Woodward's wrist. He held on, but Woodward dangled slackly in his grip, swaying with his bandanna whipping behind him.

'Tell me about her!' Jim roared.

With his eyes darkening, Woodward looked up and met Jim's gaze.

'I can't,' he murmured, his voice fading. He flashed a weak, sneering smile. 'Only Tyler knows.'

11

Jim watched Woodward's head loll. He shook him, but the man just rocked from side to side beneath him. And when he felt his own body slip another few inches down the side of the train, he had no choice but to release Woodward's body.

But first he lunged with his left hand and swiped the bandanna from Woodward's neck. Then he let Armstrong drag him back on to the roof.

'Only Tyler knows,' Armstrong intoned. 'Just what have they done to her?'

'I got no idea.' Jim fingered the bandanna, but to suppress the memories of the day he'd given this present to Zelma he slipped it into his pocket and glanced down the train roof. A half-mile ahead, he could see the station at Fall Creek. 'But I guess I

147

can't worry about that now. That ambush must be imminent.'

Armstrong nodded. With no more discussion they climbed down from the roof and returned to the end carriage. The noise they'd raised and the bodies falling from the roof had attracted the attention of the passengers, and they shied away as Jim and Armstrong headed back to their carriage.

But Jim wasn't in the mood for providing explanations and stared straight ahead.

As he reached his seat he expected a comment from Kirby's men, but he avoided looking at them and sat. He stared through the window as Woodward's comments whirled through his thoughts, but he couldn't decide whether the outlaw had played a trick on him before he died, or had admitted to something.

By the time the train pulled into Fall Creek he was no nearer to deciding the truth. So, when the train lurched to a halt, he bit back his irritation, checked that nobody was waiting on the platform, then alighted first.

Armstrong followed him out. While Jim stood on the platform he collected their horses.

Then they waited for Marshal Kirby, who still leaned back in his seat, his hat covering his face.

But just as Jim was beginning to think that the lawmen wouldn't get off the train the deputies stood one by one and, with surly glances in all directions, alighted. Two of their number led their horses from the train, then joined the others in lining up before the station wall and watching the train take on water.

Jim and Armstrong stood apart from the group.

Only when the conductor hollered that they were ready to move on out did Kirby lift his hat from his face and leave the carriage with a steady swagger. But he stood on the edge of the platform, facing away from the station.

Then the train pulled out, the wind

whipping Kirby's long coat, but he set his feet wide and stood motionless.

Jim and Armstrong exchanged glances. Then both men paced to the end of the platform and, twenty yards to Kirby's side, rested their hands on their gunbelts.

But still the deputies waited, nonchalantly removing their hats and replacing them, or just tapping a raised foot against the station wall. The only sound was distant birdcall.

When the train disappeared into the dust and heat haze, Jim's impatience overcame his irritation and he wandered down the platform, past the line of deputies. He made eye contact with each man, but they all peered back with studied insolence.

He looked into the telegraph office, but nobody was on duty. So he paced across the platform to stand beside Kirby.

'When are we heading to Clearwater?' he asked.

Kirby continued to stare across the

tracks at the barren wilderness before the station.

'My men will do what I tell them to do. You can go to hell.'

'But you must have seen the trouble I had on the train roof.'

'Yeah.'

'Well, those men were in Luther Wade's gang, and they're just a hint of what's waiting for us before we get back to Clearwater.'

Kirby feigned a huge yawn.

'And if the likes of you defeated them, they don't worry me.'

Jim took a deep breath.

'Even so, remember I can be of use to you.'

Kirby snapped an oath, but Jim turned and headed back across the platform to join Armstrong.

'Are we waiting?' Armstrong asked, his voice low. 'Or are we hiding?'

Jim opened his mouth to answer, but then lead tore into the wall above his head. He flinched away from the splinters and scrambled for his gun, but along the wall the deputies ripped out their guns and thundered gunfire in all directions.

Most of the deputies fanned out, but two of them danced out from the wall to fire up at the roof.

A cry emerged and a man who was edging over the apex tumbled down the roof to land on the platform. The line of deputies blasted down at him, ensuring he was dead, as two deputies swirled round and ripped lead through the telegraph office door.

For a moment pained screeches from within drowned out the sound of thundering lead.

Marshal Kirby himself jumped off the edge of the platform to stand astride the tracks. He fired down the track at a tangle of rocks that was just beyond the platform.

Although from his position Jim couldn't see anyone hiding there, Kirby still fired at the rocks. And, on the third shot, two men made the mistake of bobbing up to return fire, but before either man could blast off a single shot, Kirby hammered lead into the first man's guts and into the second man's head.

The second man crumpled, but as the first man staggered back from the rocks, Kirby blasted a second shot into his side that spun him around and to the ground.

Jim and Armstrong dashed out from the wall to search out other raiders as all around them the deputies maintained a furious barrage.

A second man rolled down from the roof, clutching his chest. Two more gunshots thudded into him before he slammed to the ground.

Another man made an abortive run around the side of the station, but a hail of gunfire nearly tore him in two before he'd run three paces.

Two more men emerged from behind an abandoned wagon to continue the ambush but, on seeing the sprawl of bodies, they panicked and hightailed it down the trail. Lead peppered their backs, knocking them to their knees, then to the ground.

A gunshot from behind winged past Jim's arm, but even as he swung round to face his attacker Kirby had blasted a shot between this man's eyes, wheeling him over the side of the platform and on to the tracks.

Three riders emerged from behind a thicket beside the station. Luther Wade was in their midst but, on seeing the carnage, they swung their horses round and galloped away from the station. Lead ripped into the trailing rider's back, tumbling him from his horse, and a speculative long shot winged the second man to the ground, leaving just Luther to hurtle away.

Then the gunfire ricochets echoed to silence and the only movements came from the tattered clothing of their attackers' bodies blowing in the breeze, the only sound the returning birdcall.

The deputies stood poised, each man staring in a different direction with their guns thrust out, awaiting any further attacks. But even though Jim had only known these men for an hour, he detected in their stances a confidence that suggested they didn't expect any of the raiders to still be capable of mounting an assault.

Then, to a short nod from Kirby, they holstered their guns with a collective flourish and headed down the platform to their horses.

Jim holstered his own gun, then pulled up his sleeve to see that the bullet had torn through the cloth.

Kirby stopped beside him and glanced at the bullet rip.

'Yeah,' he said, 'you are of use to me. You gave them someone else to shoot at.'

⋆ ⋆ ⋆

Outside the sheriff's office in Clearwater, only Marshal Kirby dismounted.

His deputies spread out down the road in a sprawl that, to the casual viewer, would appear undisciplined.

But after spending several hours in their company on the quiet journey back to Clearwater, Jim could see their serious intent in the way they covered all possible directions from which an attack could come.

But after the number of men they'd dispatched at Fall Creek, Jim reckoned that Luther was probably the only man out of his original gang of twenty who was still alive.

Jim dismounted and hurried to reach the office before Kirby, but Kirby had already achieved a steady momentum. He brushed him aside, then kicked open the office door.

'Hopeman,' he said, standing in the doorway, 'I've come for your man.'

Hopeman paced round to stand before Kirby.

'And I sure am glad you're here. You get any trouble on the way?'

'I didn't.' Kirby chuckled. 'But Luther Wade's gang sure did. Now, I ain't got time to waste. Where's the man who shot Benny Lawson?'

'Over here.' Hopeman gestured to the corner cell.

In the cell Tyler peered up, yawned, then leaned back against the wall with his hands clasped behind his head.

'I ain't interested in him,' Kirby said, his voice cold and sneering as he paced across the office to stand before the corner cell.

Hopeman joined Kirby. 'But he's Tyler Coleman.'

'I know that. But I'm here to collect the man who shot Benny Lawson.'

Hopeman glanced over his shoulder at Jim, his brow furrowed. Jim returned a shrug and Hopeman matched the shrug, then pointed into the cell.

'And this is him,' he intoned.

Kirby glared into the cell at Tyler, who returned the glare. Kirby shook his head and paced across the office to the doorway. He swung to a halt and waited with his head cocked to one side until Hopeman and Jim joined him.

'I don't appreciate taking journeys I

don't need,' he muttered, looking into the road.

'But I do need you to take Tyler to trial.'

'And there will be no trial.' Kirby gestured over his shoulder at Tyler. 'Because that man didn't kill Benny Lawson.'

12

'But dozens of people know he killed Benny,' Jim said as he strode outside and stood on the boardwalk.

Kirby joined Jim and spat on the ground.

'Any of those people care to explain themselves to me?'

'We don't have a live witness, but we have enough for you to take him to trial.'

'And if Judge Plummer weren't such a busy man he might enjoy hearing you explain yourself.'

'He has to spend the time.' Jim slammed his hands on his hips. 'The court must decide the truth about who killed Benny Lawson.'

'It must, but I know Tyler Coleman didn't kill him.'

Jim paced in a short circle on the boardwalk.

'How can you be so sure?'

'Because on the day *someone* killed Benny Lawson, Tyler Coleman was in jail in Green Valley, starting a five-year sentence for raiding Block Ridge's bank.'

Jim winced, then lowered his head.

'You sure?'

'Yeah, because I tracked him down for the crime, and arrested him two weeks before Benny Lawson died.'

'Two weeks!'

'And for the next five years Tyler festered in jail.' Kirby glanced through the open office door at the corner cell. 'It's my guess Tyler completed his sentence a few weeks ago and was heading off to restart his worthless life, oblivious to your belief that he committed a murder.'

'I don't understand this,' Jim murmured, tipping back his hat. 'People saw Tyler loitering around town right up until the raid and — '

'And will they swear on oath that they saw him?' Kirby stared at Jim until he glanced away. 'Or was it typical frontier-town rumour?'

'I know how rumours start. But this was different. Too many people saw . . .'

Jim sighed, shaking his head. He glanced at Hopeman for support, but Hopeman could only return a slow and sad shake of the head.

'And I'm telling you,' Kirby said, 'that anybody who claimed they saw Tyler was plain mistaken.'

Kirby stared at Jim until he gave a reluctant nod.

'I guess that is likely.'

Kirby sneered, then turned to the Lucky Star and gestured for his men to join him.

'And when you catch the man who did do it, tell me. But until then, you got no reason to hold Tyler Coleman, and I got no reason to waste my time talking to you.'

★ ★ ★

Ten miles out of Clearwater Hopeman pulled the wagon to a halt.

With a last glance at Jim, Hopeman rolled into the back of the wagon and removed the cloth he'd thrown over the bottom of the wagon to reveal the bound and hooded man beneath.

He hunkered down beside him and ripped off the hood to reveal Tyler, who cringed, then peered up, his eyes narrowed against the brightness.

Still staying quiet, Hopeman removed Tyler's handcuffs and stood back, but Tyler stayed curled.

'Get up,' Hopeman muttered.

'I ain't making this easy for you,' Tyler said, a tremor in his voice. Then he coughed and continued with a firmer voice. 'I'm an innocent man and you got no right lynching me.'

'And I ain't lynching you. I'm letting you go.'

'I don't believe that. You hooded me and dragged me out of town.'

'I did. But even if I know you're innocent, plenty more in Clearwater won't believe it. I've taken you out of town without anyone noticing. And by the time anyone does notice, you'd better be long gone.'

Tyler blinked hard, then rolled to his knees to peer over the side of the wagon. He appraised his horse, then Jim and Hopeman in turn, then the deserted trail. He shrugged then jumped down from the back of the wagon.

'This is some kind of trick, ain't it?' he said, stretching. 'You're raising my hopes, but then you'll take it all away.'

'No trick. Marshal Kirby spoke up for you. He told us you were in jail when Benny Lawson died.'

Tyler glanced away, shrugging.

'Guess I owe him a favour, then. But I got no desire to go if you'll just drag me back to Clearwater another day. I'd prefer my day in court to prove my innocence.'

'You don't need no day in no court.' Hopeman rolled into the front of the wagon and raised the reins. 'I know

now that you're innocent. All charges are dropped and you can go.'

Tyler kicked at the dirt. 'But what about — '

'Tyler,' Hopeman snapped, leaning forward in the seat to glare down at the ex-prisoner, 'I don't know what you're trying to gain out of this situation, but it won't work. I made a mistake when I arrested you. And I've put that right.'

Tyler wandered round on the spot, staring at the deserted trail behind and ahead of him, then at the barren hills.

'I ain't looking for no gain. I just want to leave Clearwater alive.'

'And you've done that.' Hopeman pointed down the trail. 'So, just get on your horse, head on down the trail, and don't ever return to my town.'

Tyler grabbed his horse's reins and looked north, but then turned and looked at Hopeman.

'What about an apology?'

Hopeman snorted then shook the reins and hurried the wagon away.

Jim stayed back, wondering how he

could question Tyler about Zelma without alerting Hopeman, but when Tyler just mounted his horse and galloped away, he turned and hurried his horse on to flank Hopeman's wagon.

For the next five miles the lawmen rode in silence, but on the edge of Caleb Lawson's land Hopeman pulled the wagon to a halt and glanced at Jim.

'Jim,' he said, his shoulders slumping, 'the new investigation into Benny's murder starts tonight.'

'Obliged. But aside from finding Luther, I don't know where to start.'

'We'll worry about that later. But now I have to explain to your father that I had to let Tyler go. I'd prefer him to hear it from me first — and alone.' Hopeman sighed. 'I reckon if you tried to explain it to him it could be another five years before he'd speak to you again.'

'I reckon so, too.' Jim flashed an encouraging smile, then kept his horse back as Hopeman headed off towards Caleb's ranch.

Jim waited until Hopeman was too far away to tell where he was going if he looked back, then turned and headed off down the trail.

He rode northwards and, within thirty minutes, reached the spot where Hopeman had freed Tyler.

Tyler had gone, but he searched for his tracks and, as there had been few travellers down this trail, picked them up with some ease. At a fair pace he followed them and, within the hour and twenty miles out of Clearwater, saw a lone rider heading away.

Jim hurried but when he was 200 yards back, the rider glanced over his shoulder then speeded.

By now Jim had confirmed that the rider was Tyler. He hailed him, but this forced Tyler to gallop off.

Jim had no choice but to settle in for the long pursuit, but with the extra distance Jim's horse had travelled Tyler rapidly increased the gap. So when

Tyler swung in an arc around a huge outcropping of rock, Jim drew his gun and fired over his head.

As the gunshot echoed back from the outcrop and the crag beyond, Tyler glanced over his shoulder. Jim fired again, his arm thrust high, clearly showing that he was only firing to attract his attention.

This time, Tyler slowed to a halt and waited for Jim. Even so, he backed towards the outcrop, seemingly ready to go for cover if Jim's intentions weren't benign, and he raised a hand to order Jim to stop when he was fifty yards away.

'Why are you following me?' he shouted.

'I got a question,' Jim shouted, pulling his horse to a halt.

Tyler slapped his thigh. 'I was right. You wouldn't really let me go.'

'I *am* letting you go.' Jim walked his horse towards Tyler, who held his ground. 'I just want to hear the truth about Benny Lawson, and about Luther

Wade, and about Zel ... about anything else you'd care to tell me.'

Tyler glared at Jim, but when Jim smiled he snorted, then nudged his horse on to meet him.

'I'll say this once, and you'd better believe it because there ain't no more. I didn't kill Benny Lawson.'

'And I believe you now.' Jim watched Tyler heave a sigh of relief. 'But why does everyone reckon you did do it?'

'Got no idea. There couldn't have been any witnesses because I never met him.'

'There was one — Monty Elwood.'

'Monty,' Tyler snorted, 'ain't a reliable witness.'

'So, you did know Monty.'

Tyler flashed a glare at Jim, but then glanced around at the deserted trail.

'Deputy, I got a long journey ahead of me, and I ain't got the time to waste talking to you. So, either arrest me or let me go, but either way, you won't ever prove I killed some man called Benny Lawson.'

'When you speak of Benny,' Jim snapped, 'remember that he was my brother and his death killed my mother and destroyed my father's life.'

Tyler winced, then lowered his head.

'I understand your need to make someone pay, but I still can't help you.'

'Then try this — I can help you avoid the person who wants to kill you.'

Tyler bit his bottom lip. 'You talking about Luther Wade?'

'Yeah. And if he's trying to kill you, it's my duty to stop him, but I need to know the full story to do that.'

Tyler sighed and swung round to look down the trail.

'Monty Elwood reckoned that Caleb . . . your father owed him five hundred dollars,' he said, his voice more relaxed than before. 'So, Luther and me agreed to steal what he was owed, but we had to leave town and we never carried through with the raid. That's all I know.'

Jim nodded. 'And why has your friendship with Luther turned sour?'

Tyler licked his lips then glanced at Jim.

'Men like him . . . like us .. don't need much of a reason.'

'And you didn't know I wanted you for Benny's murder?'

'Nope. When I rode into Clearwater, I'd planned to hole up with my three hired hard-cases and wait for Luther to find me.'

'Three?'

'You killed two in the Lucky Star. I guess the third hightailed it out of town when he saw the trouble he was facing.' Tyler turned his horse to the trail. 'Now, I'm moving on before Luther finds me.'

'Then you got less to worry about than before. Marshal Kirby killed a lot of Luther's men.'

'Obliged for the information.' Tyler stared down the trail, but then glanced back at Jim. 'But why are you helping me? I didn't kill your brother, but I ain't been on the right side of the law much in my life.'

'I'll be honest with you. Luther knows about the whereabouts of a woman.' Jim searched Tyler's eyes, but they didn't flicker with any interest. 'And I reckon you know about her, too.'

'And that woman is Zelma Hayden?'

Jim took a deep breath. 'Yeah.'

'And she's special to you?'

'She was.'

Tyler nodded, rubbing his chin. 'And was that why Armstrong kidnapped me, but you brought me back?'

'Yeah.'

'Then I guess I'm obliged to you.' Tyler glanced around, murmuring to himself, then dismounted and paced towards Jim. He stopped before his horse, then turned to stare into the plains. When he spoke his voice had none of its former arrogance. 'That must have been a hard decision.'

Jim nodded, then swung down from the saddle to stand beside Tyler.

'It was, but doing my duty has a limit. And if you won't talk, when I question Luther about Benny's murder and Zelma's disappearance he might learn that you headed north when you left Clearwater.'

Tyler snorted a laugh. 'I can see he might do that.'

'I have to know what happened to Zelma.' Jim stared at Tyler until he turned to look at him, then flashed a benign smile. 'But if I know she's alive, I got no reason to mention anything about you to Luther.'

'You got a way of talking a man round to your way of thinking. So, I'll tell you this: she's alive.' Tyler looked over Jim's shoulder at the trail as Jim sighed his relief, but then his eyes flared and his mouth fell open. 'You idiot! You don't have to find Luther. He's found us.'

Jim swirled round to see that Luther Wade was galloping towards them. As Tyler swung out to face him Luther pulled his horse to a halt in a cloud of dust, then dismounted and stormed towards them.

'Luther,' Jim said, 'stop right there!'

'Be quiet, Deputy,' Luther roared, his gaze boring into Tyler as he stomped to a halt. 'I have business with Tyler.'

Jim shook his head and paced round to confront Luther, aiming to halt this showdown, but Tyler barged Jim aside.

'It was always coming to this,' he said. 'Just back off, Deputy.'

Jim glanced from one man to the other, then shook his head.

'I want information on Zelma, and one of you will give it to me.'

Luther snorted. 'Whichever one of us is still alive in one minute will tell you.'

Jim glanced at each man in turn, but then sighed and raised his hands.

The two men stood ten yards apart. Luther was rigid, his eyes blazing.

Tyler stood casually with one leg thrust out and to the side, a smile playing on his lips.

Luther snorted a deep breath, his right eye twitching as he appraised Tyler's unconcerned demeanour. His hand shook with an uncontrolled tremor, but with a roll of his shoulders he got it under control and hunched down.

Tyler snorted a chuckle, then, with a steady hand drew his gun using just his extended fingers, and punched bullets out of his gunbelt to load.

Luther watched him, then a sneer passed over his face and his hand whirled to his gun.

Five yards to Tyler's right Jim saw Luther's intent and broke into a run. With his head down he charged into Tyler's side, knocking him over. As Luther's gunshot whistled over his head, both men went down heavily, but Jim kept the roll going, dragging his Peacemaker from its holster as he tumbled.

Luther still had time to blast another slug at them, but the shot whistled by Jim's sliding form. Then Jim slid to a halt and, lying on his side, slammed a shot up into Luther's left arm.

The blast swung Luther's arm up, half-spinning his body round. Luther staggered back a pace, then righted himself and swung round to fire down at Jim again. Lead ripped into his chest and wheeled him to the ground. He moved to get up, but a spasm contorted his face before his head slammed into the dirt.

With his gun drawn Tyler paced to Luther's side and felt his neck, then nodded to Jim.

'Obliged,' Tyler said, then held out a hand to help Jim to his feet. 'Never thought a lawman would save my life.'

'Don't get too pleased. I didn't shoot him.'

'You didn't . . . ' Tyler glanced up, then snorted.

Jim rolled over to look behind him and see a line of riders hurtling down the trail. Tyler edged back and forth, but a slug ripped past his head and with that, he dashed towards the outcrop.

13

As Tyler hurried away from Jim, the line of riders hurtled around the outcrop and headed for the crag.

Jim raised a hand to his brow to shield his eyes from the low sun and tried to discern who they were, but the men blasted a volley of lead. The first slugs were high and cannoned into the outcrop behind him, but the last slug tore through Jim's hat, and that was all the encouragement Jim needed to join Tyler in dashing for the rocky outcrop.

Gunfire tore at their heels, forcing the two men to sprint the last few yards, then fling their hands up as they dived for cover.

Both men rolled to a sprawling halt behind the nearest boulder, then extricated themselves from their tangle and glanced over the boulder.

Their attackers had gone to ground,

but from the tendrils of smoke emerging from the crag to their side their location was obvious.

'Who is this?' Tyler asked.

'Don't know, but I got news for you, Tyler. You ain't a popular person in Clearwater.'

Tyler shrugged. 'Then I guess I'm glad I got the law on my side now, even if he is stupid enough to get followed.'

'Quit complaining. They probably followed Luther.' Jim sighed. 'But I'll protect you, as I always have.'

'Me and lawmen don't exactly get on.' Tyler shrugged. 'So, leave me.'

Jim glanced up, but gunfire exploded into the rock before him, ripping shards into his face. He hurled himself to the ground.

'To be honest, I wish I could, but I have my duty.'

Tyler snorted a harsh laugh. 'Either way, I reckon we have to make a move before they get settled.'

Jim nodded. 'What's your idea?'

'Staying pinned down here won't do

us no good. So, we ambush them.' Tyler pointed to a huge rock projection, some fifty yards to their side. 'You go for that rock and get a different angle on them. I'll cover you.'

'Tyler, you don't give the orders here.'

Tyler sneered. 'Then what's your plan?'

Jim glanced around, rubbing his chin, then pointed to the rock.

'I'll go for that rock. You cover me.'

Tyler chuckled. 'That seems a good plan.'

On the count of three Jim leapt up and charged for the rock. From behind, Tyler fired up at the crag, but their attackers still risked returning gunfire and plumes of dirt ripped around him as the slugs cannoned into the ground at his heels and into the outcrop at his side.

Jim looked sideways as he ran, seeing gunsmoke rising from at least five positions on the crag beside them. Then he concentrated on his running and, with his head down, scrambled into a hollow set before the rock. He hunkered down and surveyed his new position.

Beside him, a small gully ran up the side of the outcrop with protecting boulders on either side. And if he gained sufficient height, he reckoned he could look down on the crag and perhaps gain an angle that'd let him see his attackers.

He bobbed up and blasted a volley of gunfire at the men's position, suggesting he was settling in for a long siege. Then he ducked and, on hands and knees, crawled for the gully.

But then more gunfire erupted. And this time it came from a new direction.

Jim wavered, then scrambled back into the hollow and peered over the side. Systematic firing was ripping out. From the plumes of dirt rising on the crag, this person was helping him.

Jim waved to Tyler, who returned a bemused shrug. So, Jim peered around, searching for the location of the shooter. With the echoes, it was hard to work out, but he reckoned the firing was coming from the top of the outcrop to his side. To get a clearer view he crawled back from the hollow and shuffled round the side of the rocky projection, then craned his neck to peer up the side of the outcrop.

But then a shadow fell across the ground before him. And it was growing.

He swirled round, but as he turned he saw the form of a man jumping down from the projection above him. He just had time to throw up an arm in desperate defence but then the man slammed on to his back, knocking him to his knees.

He floundered on the ground, winded, and before he could extricate himself, cold metal pressed into the back of his neck.

'Stay down, Deputy,' a gruff voice ordered.

With no choice, Jim lay flat. Around him, gunfire exploded, but the sounds were intermittent.

Then people shouted, Tyler included, then another burst of gunfire, then silence.

Footfalls paced away from him and Jim strained his neck to look back. Lead tore into the earth beside his left ear and Jim slammed his face into the dirt.

Somebody shouted then hoofs thundered. This time Jim risked looking around.

The man who had jumped him had gone and out on the plains a line of riders was hurtling down the trail towards Clearwater.

Fingering the lump on the back of his head, Jim staggered to his feet, swayed, then used a hand on the rocky projection to right himself.

He staggered round the side of the projection and shuffled into the hollow, then glanced over the side, but still no gunfire arrived.

He staggered out from the hollow and dashed to Tyler's position. He found a single spot of blood on the ground, and scuffed earth, perhaps from a struggle.

A return to Clearwater to organize a rescue attempt was pressing, but somebody had tried to help him by firing down from the outcrop to his side. And Jim reckoned this was the third time in the last two days that an unknown person had helped him when he was in trouble. So Jim headed to the gully and, with his head down, climbed, gradually speeding as his grogginess receded.

He quickly gained enough height to see the surrounding area, but he was only interested in reaching the tangle of rocks that coated the apex of the outcrop. They were as barren and seemingly devoid of life as all the rocks on the outcrop were.

But he circled round to keep out of sight of these rocks until the last moment, then stood and in full view paced towards them. But he still kept his gun holstered as he slowed to a halt and stood facing them, about twenty yards back.

For a full minute he stood listening for any noise above the gentle wind rustling past him. Then he heard a faint neighing. It came from the other side of the outcrop. Jim smiled to himself and risked voicing the wild thoughts that he'd kept at bay since Max Malloy had uttered his bizarre last words.

'Monty Elwood,' he said, 'come on out.'

He waited with his arms folded, but only heard the horse again.

'I know you're alive,' he continued. 'I know you feigned your own death. The only question on my mind is why.'

For a full minute he waited. Then a man stood from behind the rocks. He was grizzled and old, but the eyes that peered out from above the matted beard were lively.

And it *was* Monty Elwood.

'How did you figure that out, Deputy?' he asked.

'Tyler Coleman's third hired gun saw you. You thought he was going to kill you because you'd claimed that Tyler killed my brother. So, you shot him, swapped clothes and, with Gene's help, you've been lying low.'

Monty nodded and paced out from behind the boulder and across the top of the outcrop until he stood before Jim.

'And am I under arrest?'

'Being alive ain't a crime, and as you've tried to save my life three times, I guess I got time to hear your side of the story.'

Monty held his hands wide, signifying that Jim should look him up and down.

'Ain't much to say other than I've been living on my wits. And now, I don't want whiskey no more and I got me some self-respect.'

Jim chuckled on seeing Monty smile for the first time that he could remember.

'I guess you have at that. Armstrong McGiven gave me hint of the man you once were, and perhaps you can be that man again.' Jim removed the smile. 'But it still leaves the question of what happened five years ago.'

Monty narrowed his eyes. 'You sure you want to hear about that?'

'I've heard plenty of half-truths and pieced together some truths.' Jim paced in a short circle, ending with him standing beside Monty and looking towards Clearwater. 'My father owed you money and you were so desperate you hired Tyler Coleman and Luther Wade to steal it back. But when Sheriff Hopeman ran Luther Wade out of town, Tyler didn't have the guts to do the raid on his own. Then Max Malloy overheard your plan and went through with it himself, except he stole everything that my father owned.'

Monty sighed. 'That pretty much sums it up.'

'But I don't know why you didn't tell everyone the truth straight away.'

'Max stopped me.'

'How?'

Monty patted Jim's shoulder. 'Believe me. You don't want to know.'

185

Jim closed his eyes and took a deep breath.

'I've gathered that Zelma had something to do with it. But I have to know the truth.'

For long moments Monty didn't reply and when he did, his voice was low and resigned.

'Zelma kept Caleb . . . ' Monty coughed and glanced away. 'She kept your father *occupied* while Max stole his money.'

Jim blinked hard, his former grogginess returning to almost tumble him to his knees. He looked skywards as he took deep breaths to calm himself.

'I can't believe that.'

'I'm afraid so. Zelma wanted excitement, and I guess helping Max provided that. But she regretted what she'd done and couldn't face you, so she left town.'

'I'd have forgiven her,' Jim gasped.

'She didn't know that. She pleaded with me to keep her secret, but Benny was all set to work it out. So I led him

186

in the wrong direction, but he got killed in Black Pass. Afterwards, Max threatened to reveal Zelma's role if I talked. So I let Caleb persuade everyone that Tyler did it.'

With a hand to his heart, Jim got his ragged breathing under control and turned to Monty.

'And who did kill Benny?'

'It wasn't Tyler, or Luther, or Max, or me.' Monty flashed a smile. 'And it wasn't Zelma.'

Jim raised his eyebrows, but when Monty just stared back at him he laid a friendly hand on his shoulder.

'These secrets have nearly ruined you, but Max Malloy is dead now and you got yourself a second chance. But you won't sort out your life until you tell the full truth.'

'I will tell you.' Monty rolled his gaze up to look at Jim. 'But only when Tyler is dead.'

'I need to know now.' Unbidden, Jim closed his hand, clamping it tight around Monty's shoulder and making him wince. 'Benny was my brother.'

'I know, but if I tell you, it'll help you save Tyler, and I can't let that happen.'

'Why?'

'Because I was an honest man before Tyler persuaded me to steal. Then I got involved with Max. Then Zelma . . . Zelma did what she did. Then she left you. Then Benny died. Then your mother died. Then you and Caleb fell out. Then . . . ' Monty shrugged out from Jim's grip and paced away to stand on the edge of the outcrop and peer out on to the plains. 'I've been doing a whole heap of thinking out here. And I reckon my life, and Caleb's life, and yours ended the moment I met Tyler. Everything that happened is his fault. And as soon as he's dead, I reckon we can all restart our lives.'

Jim joined Monty on the edge of the outcrop.

'We all make our own hells, and letting someone kill a man won't help any of us. Only I can choose to move on and forget Zelma. Only my father can forgive himself for cheating on my mother. And only *you* can tell the truth and regain your self-respect.'

'Fine words, Deputy.' Monty shuffled round to look at Jim. 'But I'll wait out here until Tyler's dead. Then I'll return to Clearwater and restart my life.'

Jim backed away a pace. 'Only the truth can help you. The quicker you deliver that, the quicker you'll start living.'

Jim stared at Monty, but on receiving only a shake of the head, he turned and, without looking back, headed down the outcrop.

Once he was down on the plains, he mounted his horse and headed back to Clearwater at a gallop.

As he rode, he had at last to admit to himself that he had to talk to Hopeman.

But what he would say refused to become any clearer on his long journey back.

The sun was dipping towards the horizon when Jim galloped into Clearwater. He dismounted outside the sheriff's office and went straight inside. Hopeman and Armstrong were drinking coffee. They both looked up.

'I got something to tell you,' Jim said, squaring up to Hopeman. 'And it ain't good.'

Hopeman invited him to come closer, but Jim stood with an almost military bearing with his chin held aloft.

'Relax, Jim,' Hopeman said. 'Nothing you can say will be as bad as meeting Marshal Kirby.'

Jim rolled his shoulders, but then relaxed his stance a mite. In the last hour, he'd considered telling him many different versions of his actions over the last two days, but it was only as he faced Sheriff Hopeman that he decided he had to provide the truth.

As briskly as he could he relayed his attempt to gain information about Zelma by going to Luther's camp, about the snippets of information he had learned about her, about his attempt to persuade Tyler to tell him what had happened, about the showdown he'd let Luther and Tyler have, and about his failure to stop somebody kidnapping Tyler.

Armstrong stared at him throughout this tale, but despite his resolution to tell the truth, Jim didn't mention Armstrong's attempt to free Tyler last night. And as Monty's planned resurrection was something personal to Monty, he avoided mentioning that and instead relayed the information about Max's and Zelma's involvement in the events of five years ago as being his own supposition.

Throughout, Hopeman remained tight-lipped.

'If you want to dismiss me,' Jim said, ending his story, 'I'll understand.'

'I can't say you did right, but you should have told me about Zelma.'

Jim tipped back his hat and glanced at Armstrong, but Armstrong was wandering towards the window, shaking his head.

'I couldn't. I didn't know whether her disappearance was personal or official business. I had to piece together whether she was involved in Benny's murder before I said anything.'

'You could have told me as a friend,' Hopeman said, his voice hurt. 'I'd have understood.' Hopeman stared at Jim until he nodded, then slapped his thighs and stood. 'But that ain't important now. I guess we need to search for Tyler.'

'But where?' Armstrong said from the window. 'It'll be dark when we get to the crag and he'll be dead long before — '

The door crashed open and Deputy Newell dashed in, waving a slip of paper above his head.

'I got news,' he said between breathless gasps, 'Marshal Kirby's sent a message to Fall Creek.'

Hopeman closed his eyes, a sigh escaping his lips.

192

'I guess it's more abuse.'

Newell shook his head, then glanced down at the slip of paper in his hand and read from it.

'It ain't. He wants to know whether you need help with your prisoner.'

'What prisoner?' Hopeman murmured.

'The message doesn't say,' Newell said, shrugging. 'It just reads — '

'Wait!' Hopeman took the message from Newell and read it, then passed the message to Jim, who confirmed that it was just as confusing as Newell had suggested.

'But Marshal Kirby has only just left Clearwater,' Jim said. 'He couldn't have returned to Green Valley by now.'

'Perhaps an earlier message got delayed,' Hopeman said. 'And we've only just got it.'

'No,' Newell said. 'The message got sent this afternoon and knowing it was urgent — '

'Damnation,' Hopeman murmured. He snatched the message from Jim, read it again, then slapped his forehead. 'I know what it means.'

Jim watched as Hopeman paced to the window, crunched the paper into a tight ball, then hurled it away. Jim considered the message and even though there was only one explanation for it, his guts rumbled with the terrible realization that the unlikely explanation was, in fact, the only explanation.

He joined Hopeman and the two men stared into the road.

'And I know what it means, too,' he murmured. 'The man who ordered us to release Tyler Coleman wasn't Marshal Kirby.'

14

'An outlaw wouldn't intercept a message meant for Marshal Kirby,' Armstrong said as he joined Jim at the window, 'then pose as him.'

'Luther's direct approach *is* more normal,' Jim murmured.

'So,' Hopeman said, 'Tyler's alibi is false, but who else would go to that much trouble?'

Jim took a deep breath, the sharp intake making the other lawmen look at him.

'I still think Tyler is innocent,' he murmured. 'But I reckon that bogus Marshal Kirby kidnapped him.'

'That's my guess, too.'

'But I know that for a fact.' Jim sighed. 'Because I didn't deliver your message yesterday.'

Hopeman winced. 'You didn't deliver — '

'I made sure it got through, all right.' Jim flashed an apologetic smile. 'My father took the message for me.'

'Caleb Lawson took the message,' Hopeman intoned.

'Or in this case, took a different message to a different person.'

Hopeman nodded. 'I guess it was inevitable he'd try to lynch Tyler. Only question is, where did he take him?'

Jim turned to the door.

'And I reckon we all know where that is.'

$\star$ $\star$ $\star$

Jim crawled to the edge of the slope and peered down into Black Pass. Down below was the tree that marked the spot where Benny had died.

'You sure this is the right place?' Armstrong asked.

'It's the only place where my father would want to lynch Tyler. We just got to wait, and he'll come.'

Armstrong glanced to the horizon,

where deep red clouds surrounded the flattened orb of the sun.

'And by sundown is my guess.'

Hopeman nodded and, with Newell, took a position thirty yards to Jim's left while Jim and Armstrong shuffled to the edge of the pass and lay on their bellies.

'You were quiet,' Jim said, 'when I told Hopeman about my suspicions.'

'I had nothing to add.'

'Not even about Monty?'

'What you mean?' Armstrong turned to look at Jim, but when Jim just stared back, he shrugged. 'He made me promise not to reveal that he was alive.'

'And I won't reveal that either. But once we've saved Tyler, he will tell me everything he knows about Benny's death, whether he wants to or not.'

Armstrong nodded. 'And do you think Tyler will tell you about Zelma?'

Jim slapped the rock before his face.

'Yeah. When Kirby ambushed us Tyler was all set to . . .' Jim rubbed his chin as he swung his head to the side to consider Armstrong. 'I've never had a proper answer from you on why you're so mighty keen to help me locate Zelma.'

Armstrong's eyes darted around the pass below as he shrugged.

'You're my friend. I want to help you.'

'But your devotion to helping me is more than I'd expect from a man I've only known for two days.'

'Some of Monty has rubbed off on me,' Armstrong said, his voice sounding hurt. 'He'd do anything for a friend.'

'And so would I, but . . . ' Jim slapped his forehead, his mind whirling as he pieced together something that he now realized should have been obvious to him. He lowered his voice. 'Tell me the truth, Armstrong.'

'About what?' Armstrong murmured.

'Zelma left town after Max Malloy robbed my father. But some people said they saw her leave with a travelling salesman.' Jim gulped. 'And that man was you.'

Armstrong stared down into the pass, not meeting Jim's gaze.

'That's a big surmise.'

'And there's more. After you stole her away from me, she left you. You reckoned that Luther Wade knew where she'd gone. So, when you arrived in Clearwater you weren't here to attend Monty's funeral, you were following Luther in your quest to find her. And when you kidnapped Tyler, you weren't trying to help me, you were trying to find her for yourself.'

'That's a mighty fine story.'

Jim slammed his fist on the rock before him, then jumped to his feet.

'It ain't no story. It's the only possible explanation for your actions. Now, tell me the truth, damn you.'

Armstrong glanced up at Jim and gulped as he fingered his beard.

'Then I guess I can't deny it. Everything you said is true.'

Jim slammed his hands on his hips and bent double to glare down at Armstrong.

'Then why not just tell me before?'

Armstrong rolled back on his haunches, then stood and squared up to Jim.

'How can you tell a friend that you now love the woman he once loved?'

'You can't,' Jim shouted. He hurled his hands above his head, his outburst attracting Hopeman's and Newell's attention. 'But lying was wrong.'

'You're angry. I can see that, but — '

'I sure am!' Jim stabbed a firm finger at Armstrong's chest. 'Why did you steal my woman?' Jim slammed his finger with more power, forcing Armstrong to back a pace, then continued punctuating his points with more stabs. 'Why did you return to taunt me? Why did you lie to me? And why did you steal my life?'

'I did none of those things.' Armstrong snorted as Jim slammed his finger again. This time he threw up a hand and grabbed Jim's, then twisted it down to his side and pushed Jim back a pace. A hint of anger flashed in his eyes. 'But do you really want the truth?'

'Yeah,' Jim grunted, squaring up to Armstrong. 'Let me hear it.'

'Then I'll tell you.' Armstrong raised his eyebrows. 'Zelma said you were boring. And I gave her the excitement — '

'Enough!' Jim roared and charged Armstrong. At full speed he slammed into his ribs and knocked him back three paces before the two men tumbled to the ground.

They tussled, anger fuelling Jim's wild blows as he worked off his frustration of the last few days.

But before he could inflict any damage on Armstrong's body, Hopeman and Newell scurried along the top of the pass and leapt on them, then dragged them apart.

'Stop that, Jim!' Hopeman roared, taking a firm grip of Jim's arms. 'You're a lawman, and we're trying to save a man from a lynching.'

Jim struggled to free himself, but then

stood tall and lunged at Armstrong. The blow whistled through the air, but fell way short.

'He stole my woman.'

'If what you said is right, you'd already lost Zelma when she . . . she dallied with your father.'

'I'd have forgiven her. And I got every right to pound Armstrong's ugly hide into the ground.'

'You have, but this ain't the right time.' Hopeman swung Jim round to face him and, with his hands clamped on both shoulders, stared into his eyes. 'Is it, Deputy?'

'I guess this ain't the best time to start a fight,' Jim murmured.

With Jim's more conciliatory tone, Hopeman relaxed his grip, but Jim used the opportunity to hurl out his arms and throw Hopeman away from him. Then he swirled round and stormed two long paces.

With Newell still holding Armstrong rigid, he slammed a firm blow to Armstrong's cheek. The blow rocked

Armstrong's head to the side and was strong enough to tumble both Newell and Armstrong to the ground.

'Stop that!' Hopeman snapped, advancing on Jim from behind.

But the blood was still boiling in Jim's head and he dragged Armstrong to his feet and, with a round-armed punch to the chin, grounded him, then stood over him.

'If you reckon you're man enough to steal my woman, prove you got the guts to fight for her.'

'I got the guts,' Armstrong murmured, fingering a trickle of blood dribbling into his beard as he glared up at Jim. 'After all the trouble we've faced together, you know that.'

'I just know I thought you were helping me because you were my friend. But you were just feeling guilty.'

Armstrong shook his head. 'Nothing you can say will make me fight you.'

'Then try this: if life with you was so exciting, why isn't Zelma with you now?'

Armstrong's eyes blazed. With a huge roar he leapt to his feet and charged Jim. Bent double and leading with his shoulder, he hammered into Jim's waist. His solid force wheeled Jim back five paces until Jim's foot slipped and they both rolled over each other.

Jim heard Newell's and Hopeman's exasperated complaints but his mind was oblivious to everything but trying to slug the man he'd thought was his friend into oblivion.

He threw up berserk blow after berserk blow, Armstrong defending himself by throwing wild punch after wild punch back. They rolled into a boulder, then rolled back, dust flying around them as they fought.

But then Armstrong got a firm grip of Jim's collar and, on his back, wheeled him over his head to land behind him.

Jim lay winded, but when he staggered to his feet, it was to see Hopeman leap between them.

'Jim,' he grunted, 'they're coming.'

'Nothing you can say will stop me beating that man into a pulp.'

'They are coming!' Hopeman shouted again.

Jim still moved to push Hopeman aside, but then Hopeman's words filtered through his angerfuelled mind and he lowered his fist. Armstrong, too, looked round.

Below them, a troop of riders was heading into the pass. At the front rode the bound and gagged Tyler Coleman.

Armstrong and Jim leapt to the ground to take up their previous positions. Hopeman glanced at them both, shaking his head, but then joined Newell further down the pass.

'Don't go thinking I'm finished with you,' Jim murmured from the corner of his mouth.

Armstrong swirled round to glare at him. His mouth opened, but he bit back whatever he'd planned to say and looked down the slope at the approaching riders.

Below them, Tyler was bound on a

horse. At his side, Caleb had the horse on a tight rein, and following them was the bogus Marshal Kirby and his supposed deputies.

They pulled up before the solitary tree within the pass and Kirby helped Caleb to hurl a rope over the thickest branch. They secured it then tied the end into a noose and dragged it over Tyler's head.

Then, in front of the horse, Caleb fell to his knees. He ranted and wailed. He shook his fist at Tyler. He berated Tyler with a stream of invective, but Tyler stared aloft, seemingly beyond hope that Caleb would believe his story that he was innocent.

On the edge of the slope, the lawmen viewed the scene, confirming that it was exactly what it appeared to be. Then Jim slipped back from the edge to join Hopeman.

'I don't like the look of this,' he said. 'I reckon my father has finally lost his mind.'

'He hasn't,' Hopeman said, then

raised his eyebrows and looked at Jim. 'He's just angry, and when men are angry, they do wild things.'

Feeling suitably chastised, Jim glanced at Armstrong and the two men exchanged a frown and a shrug. Then Hopeman moved to stand, but Jim shook his head and gestured for him to stay down.

He stood and took steady paces down the slope.

'Father,' he shouted, 'give him up.'

Caleb continued to rant at Tyler, but Kirby hailed him, then pointed up the slope. Caleb still vented his anger at Tyler and Kirby had to pull Caleb away from Tyler's horse, then point him towards Jim.

Caleb winced and hung his head, then shook his fist at Jim.

'Stay away, Jim,' he roared, his voice echoing down the pass. 'I'm handing out justice for Benny like you should have done.'

'This ain't justice and if you kill a man in cold blood, you'll suffer the same fate. And I don't want to lose another member of my family.'

'You lost me five years ago.' Caleb paced around Tyler's horse with his hand raised and ready to slap its rump and chase it away from the tree.

Jim winced, then broke into a run down the slope, but Kirby spat to the side, then swung round, arcing his gun towards Jim. In self-preservation, Jim leapt to the ground as Kirby's first shot whistled over his tumbling form.

Kirby blasted sustained gunfire, forcing Jim to scramble for cover on his knees behind the nearest rock. He could hear his father calling for Kirby to halt his onslaught and, by degrees, the gunfire petered out.

Jim peered down the slope to see that the gunfire had spooked Tyler's horse and it was edging back and forth, straining the noose around Tyler's neck.

He heard Hopeman's subdued tones at the top of the slope as he ordered Armstrong and Newell to aim for positions down the slope and closer to

Tyler and Caleb. In a line, they ventured over the edge of the slope.

Again, Kirby fired up at them, but this time Jim swung his gun on top of the rock and blasted covering gunfire. When this forced Kirby and his men to scurry for cover behind the numerous boulders in the pass, he jumped to his feet, then vaulted the rock before him and hurtled down the slope.

Kirby and his men took it in turns to bob up and hammer lead at him, but he thrust his head down and pounded down the slope as fast as he could, zigzagging every time he reckoned another shot was imminent. Armstrong and Newell were ten paces behind him. Hopeman scurried in a long arc to gain a position twenty yards to his left.

Caleb was yelling at Kirby to desist, but Jim didn't put all his faith in his success. Ten yards from the bottom of the pass, he leapt to the ground to skid on his belly, gaining the minimal cover of a hollow, the higher position keeping him from Kirby's view.

There he lay, getting his breath, then he ventured a glance down the slope, but gunfire tore into the earth before his face and he ducked again.

'Enough, Father,' Jim shouted. 'However much you hate Tyler, you can't control those hired guns, and I know you don't want to be responsible for my death.'

'Then back off,' Caleb shouted.

'I can't. I have to get justice for Benny.' Jim took a deep breath. 'And Benny would have wanted proper justice in a real court, too. He respected the law. And he died defending it.'

'Don't speak to me about the law,' Caleb roared. 'If you were half the man Benny was, you'd have caught Tyler five years ago.'

'And you're right.' Jim looked up. 'Benny would have made a better lawman than I could ever be.'

Caleb slammed his hands on either side of his head and roared his frustration. His pained shout echoed back and forth across the pass and, when it faded to oblivion, he looked up at Jim.

'I'm sorry, Jim,' he shouted, then raised his hand to slap Tyler's horse. 'But I have to do this.'

'Don't,' Jim shouted. 'I know about Zelma.'

Caleb flinched, then lowered his hand. 'Zelma?'

'I know you went with her. I know you're obsessed with killing Tyler to avoid facing the truth.'

'What truth?'

Jim gulped. 'That your weakness lost you your money, and Benny died trying to get it back.'

'You will not accuse me of that,' Caleb roared, then swung back his hand.

Hopeman leapt up and fired a warning shot down the slope at him, but Kirby also leapt up and his gunfire forced Hopeman to dive for cover. Jim and Armstrong also tried to return fire, but Kirby's men kept them pinned down with a barrage of gunfire.

But then gunfire exploded from further down the pass.

Jim peered up to see a lone rider heading into the pass, his gun thrust out and firing. The man blasted a high shot into the chest of one of Kirby's men which wheeled him over a boulder, then a second shot that slammed another man to the dirt.

Caleb stood by the horse for a moment, then leapt to the ground in self-preservation.

Fifty yards back from the hanging-tree, the rider skidded his horse to a halt, his gun raised and aimed at Caleb.

As Jim stared at the old and grizzled rider a smile emerged.

The rider was Monty Elwood.

15

'Monty,' Caleb murmured, 'you're . . . you're alive.'

'I am now,' Monty said, roving his gun over the boulders behind which Kirby and his men were hiding.

'But how?'

'Answering that ain't going to sort this out. Now, step away from Tyler. He's guilty of just about everything a man can do, but he didn't kill your son.'

In wide-eyed shock, Caleb stared at Monty, but then, with a shake of his head, he regained his composure.

'I don't know what you're trying to prove with this trick,' he snapped, pointing up at Monty, then got up on his feet and took a determined pace towards Tyler. 'But I've waited five years to have my revenge on Tyler Coleman, and nobody can tell me he didn't kill Benny.'

Monty edged his horse forwards so that he was twenty yards from Caleb and level with Kirby, then lowered his head and his voice.

'I can.'

'But you saw Tyler do it.'

Monty swung his horse round to advance between Caleb and Tyler, but Caleb took another pace and raised his hand to slap the horse.

In response, Monty lowered his gun and flashed a smile, encouraging Caleb to lower his hand.

'I didn't. Tyler didn't kill Benny.'

'Then who did?'

'The man who killed Benny *was* Benny.'

Caleb gulped. 'What you getting at?'

'I'm getting at the truth. It was an accident, a terrible accident.'

Caleb staggered back a pace. 'You can't change your story now.'

'I'm not. I never said it *was* Tyler. You put words into my mouth and I went along with them. It was better than telling the truth when Tyler would never return.'

'Benny was a fine shot. He wouldn't shoot himself by accident.'

'But he did. And you have to accept that. You tell everybody that Benny was a great man and that he would have achieved great things, but — '

'He would have.'

'And perhaps he would. But even great men learn from the stupid things they do when they're young. But Benny didn't get the second chance to learn that a gun can be more dangerous to its owner than its target.'

Caleb's gun fell from his slack fingers and he crumpled to his knees. He knelt with his head bowed then peered up at Monty.

'What happened?' he murmured, his voice broken and defeated.

'Benny charged into the pass, his gun drawn and ready to take anybody. I told him to be cautious and to holster his gun until he saw trouble. But he saw trouble behind every bush and every boulder. He fired left. He fired right. He fired over his shoulder. And then he fell from his horse. Somehow, he shot himself in the leg. Never thought a man could bleed to death from a leg wound, but the blood kept gushing out, and he died.'

'How can I trust you?'

'I got nothing to gain from lying.' Monty glanced up the slope at Jim. 'And everything to gain by telling the truth.'

Caleb bowed his head so deeply his forehead pressed to the dirt. A single sob escaped his lips. Then he looked up, the fire that had burned in his eyes extinguished.

'Then I guess I've heard the truth. Jim's right. My weakness got Benny killed.' He glanced to the side at Kirby's position. 'And this is over.'

'Caleb,' Kirby muttered from behind his covering boulder, 'you paid us to complete a job.'

'I did, but I don't want that job done no more.'

'You might not, but I lost good men over this.'

Kirby leapt up and scythed an arc of gunfire across Caleb's chest, staggering him back two paces and into Tyler's horse, clutching his guts.

As the horse jostled back and forth, the motion rocking Tyler to the extent of his noose, Monty roared his anger and charged Kirby's position. Monty vaulted the boulder, forcing Kirby to throw himself flat, then drew his horse to a halt, turned, and hurtled back at Kirby.

Up the slope, Jim rocked back on his haunches, staring in horror at his father lying flat on his back, but he bit back his shock and jumped to his feet. With his head down, he hurtled towards the bottom of the pass.

Kirby still had two men and they leapt up and fired up the slope. At Jim's side, Armstrong and Newell also hurtled down the slope. Hopeman was to his left. All the lawmen fired on the run, forcing Kirby's men

217

to dive for cover.

But as Hopeman vaulted down to the pass's bottom, one of Kirby's men risked returning fire.

Jim dived to the ground, Armstrong and Newell also going to their knees, but Hopeman stayed on his feet and the hail of gunfire ripped across his chest, wheeling him to the ground.

Jim rolled over a shoulder and came up charging forwards, firing on the run. His first two shots were wild but his next shot ripped into the man who had shot Hopeman, slamming him on to his back.

The man ploughed through the dirt before coming to a halt, but from the ground, he hammered a high shot into Newell's chest, spinning the deputy to the ground. Then he turned his gun towards Jim, but before he could fire, Jim planted a slug in the man's forehead.

Then he sprinted towards the second man. Beside him, Monty was bearing down on Kirby.

On one knee, Kirby readied his aim and fired up. The blow skimmed past Monty's shoulder and forced him to duck and veer his horse away.

But by Tyler's horse, Caleb thrust up a hand and, with a weak and desperate shot, fired at Kirby. The shot was wild, but it made Kirby flinch and, in that moment of indecision, Monty tore his horse to the side and bore down on him at a gallop.

Monty hammered lead into Kirby's shoulder, knocking him into the boulder behind him. With his back braced against the boulder Kirby stood upright and returned fire. From only yards away the lead tore into his horse's neck and dragged a pained screech from the animal as it threw Monty to the ground.

To Jim's side Armstrong was running towards this fight and, as Kirby took careful aim at the sprawling Monty, Armstrong slammed lead into Kirby's belly, knocking him to the side. A second shot hammered him flat. And a third shot ensured he'd never get up again.

Jim continued to advance on the sole standing man, but, after winging a shot past the man's head, his Peacemaker clicked with a fatal emptiness.

The man grinned and steadied his aim on him, but then staggered back and around as lead ripped into his chest. He fell to his knees, but as he forced his gun arm to rise, a second shot to the back keeled him over to slam his face into the dirt.

Jim glanced around, then saw Armstrong standing with his gun raised. And behind him, he saw Monty lying beside his horse, his gun trained on the shot man.

'Obliged,' Jim said.

'No problem,' Armstrong said, 'for a friend.'

'And no problem,' Monty said, 'for a man who attended my funeral.'

16

Jim hurried past Monty and Armstrong to his father's side, but Caleb was sitting up, a hand clamped over his chest.

'Bullet's not in me,' he grunted. 'It busted a rib, but I'll be fine.'

Jim nodded. 'I'll get you back to Clearwater and get you fixed up.'

Caleb flashed a smile through gritted teeth.

'And as I'm in some pain, I'd be obliged if you don't take too long getting Tyler out of that noose.'

Jim glanced at the Tyler's horse, seeing that it was still spooked and jigging back and forth, forcing Tyler to strain in the saddle to avoid being torn away. He jumped to his feet and grabbed the reins, then talked calmly to the horse, stilling it, while Armstrong untied the noose from the tree.

Tyler jumped down and, when Armstrong severed his bonds, rubbed his neck and gave a huge whoop. But Jim didn't wait for his thanks and dashed around the pass checking that Kirby's men were as dead as he'd presumed.

Armstrong and Monty checked on Newell and Hopeman, confirming that they were dead, too. They stood over the bodies with their heads bowed, but with the urgency of returning his father to Clearwater, Jim ordered them to round up the horses. Then he hunkered down beside Caleb.

'I guess there'll be consequences,' Caleb said.

'There always are.'

'But whatever happens, I'm sorry. I never thought you were a bad lawman for not finding Benny's killer.' Caleb flashed a weak smile. 'I just couldn't face you after I ruined all our lives by going with Zelma, and I . . . '

Jim shook his head. 'I ain't interested in hearing about the past no more. I just want a future.'

Caleb nodded and patted Jim's arm. 'Then perhaps . . . perhaps you could come round for dinner sometime and we can talk.'

'I'd like that, but only on one condition.' Jim watched Caleb raise his eyebrows. 'You explain everything to Mother.'

Caleb snapped his eyes shut. 'I can't do that.'

'Just because she's dead, it doesn't mean you have to cut her out of your life. I visit her and Benny every week and tell them what I've been doing, and I know she'll forgive you.'

Caleb opened his eyes, then swiped away the moisture that was threatening to brim over.

'How can you know that?'

Jim patted Caleb's shoulder. 'Because I do.'

Caleb bit back a sob, but to give his father a moment alone Jim stood and turned. He saw that Armstrong had already secured two horses and was leading them down the pass. Jim joined him.

'You and him fine now?' Armstrong asked.

'We will be.' Jim edged from foot to foot as he searched for the right words to apologize for his former anger, but Armstrong smiled and held his hands wide.

'If you want to hit me because I stole your woman,' he said, 'I won't fight you this time. I ain't angry no more.'

Jim glanced around at the slew of bodies.

'Yeah. Fights like this make you realize who your real friends are.'

'They sure do.' Armstrong pointed over Jim's shoulder at Tyler Coleman, who was leading the horse on which Caleb had planned to hang him towards them. 'But what are you going to do about him?'

Jim turned to face Tyler, a faint smile on his lips.

'Yeah,' Jim said, 'what am I going to do about you?'

'Like I told you,' Tyler said. 'I'm guilty of plenty of things, but I had nothing to do with what happened here.'

'I know. But you do owe me the truth about Zelma Hayden.' Jim pointed at Tyler. 'And after all the trouble I've gone through to keep you alive, you will tell me.'

Tyler glanced at Armstrong and flashed a smile, then lowered his head.

'I don't know much.' He gulped and lowered his voice to a whisper. 'She left me.'

'She left you?' Jim blurted, then slapped a hand to his face. He peered at Armstrong through the splayed fingers. 'Does Tyler mean that after you stole her off me, he stole her off you?'

'I didn't,' Tyler said before Armstrong could answer. 'But Woodward did.'

'Woodward!' Jim and Armstrong murmured together.

'Yeah,' Tyler said. 'She went from Armstrong to Woodward, then from Woodward to Luther, then from Luther to me. Why do you think Luther

225

wanted to kill me?'

'And then she left you?' Jim asked as he watched Monty lead the remaining horses to the bottom of the pass.

'Yeah, she said life with me just wasn't exciting enough. The last I heard, she was heading north to Block Ridge.' Tyler tipped his hat. 'And as that's all I can tell you, I reckon I'll leave now. Other people in Clearwater could still want to deliver justice to me.'

'I guess they could, but I've done a lot to keep you alive. Make my efforts mean something and try to stay out of trouble.'

'I was trying to do that when I rode into Clearwater.' Tyler mounted his horse and swung round to pass by them. 'But I'll try harder next time.'

Jim watched Tyler ride past the hanging-tree, then went to Caleb's side. With Armstrong taking his father's left arm and Monty bustling around them, they levered him to his feet, then walked him to his horse.

'Were you two fighting over Zelma,

too?' Caleb said as they stood him straight beside his horse.

'We were,' Jim said. 'But once you're in good hands, I'll buy him a whiskey to show we got no hard feelings.'

Armstrong shook his head. 'Thanks for the offer, but I'm moving on now I have the information I wanted.'

Jim frowned, but then nodded. 'That Zelma was heading north towards Block Ridge?'

'Yeah. Even after everything she's done, I still want to find her. And I reckon this time, I'll — '

'But she left you,' Jim blurted.

'Yeah, but Zelma's a beguiling woman.' Armstrong's eyes glazed, perhaps with an old memory. 'And there ain't nothing you can say that will stop me trying to find her.'

Monty coughed and patted Armstrong's shoulder.

'But what if I were to tell you,' he said with a gaptoothed smile, 'that me and her once had something special going?'

'You and her?' Armstrong murmured, looking Monty's grizzled form up and down.

Monty shrugged. 'Like you said: she was a beguiling woman. And with — '

'Enough!' Armstrong shouted, slapping his hands over his ears. He lowered his head and stared at the ground, then sighed and shared eye-contact with Jim. 'Come on, Jim. You were right. We got some drinking to do to an old friend that we . . . that a lot of us knew.'

Jim nodded and, with that agreement, they levered Caleb on to his horse. Jim waited while Caleb sat tall and confirmed that he could ride, then headed to his own horse. But before he mounted it, he glanced down the pass to see that Tyler was now a good half-mile away as he rode on to the plains, his long shadow playing out beside him.

Tyler's gait was slow, but Jim couldn't help but notice that he was heading north.

We do hope that you have enjoyed reading this large print book.

Did you know that all of our titles are available for purchase?

We publish a wide range of high quality large print books including:
Romances, Mysteries, Classics
General Fiction
Non Fiction and Westerns

Special interest titles available in large print are:
The Little Oxford Dictionary
Music Book, Song Book
Hymn Book, Service Book

Also available from us courtesy of Oxford University Press:
Young Readers' Dictionary
(large print edition)
Young Readers' Thesaurus
(large print edition)

For further information or a free brochure, please contact us at:
Ulverscroft Large Print Books Ltd.,
The Green, Bradgate Road, Anstey,
Leicester, LE7 7FU, England.
Tel: (00 44) **0116 236 4325**
Fax: (00 44) **0116 234 0205**

Other titles in the
Linford Western Library:

ROPE JUSTICE

Ben Coady

Dan Brady is resting at a creek when, hearing a commotion on the opposite side of the water, he discovers a lynching in progress. Brady's sense of justice spurs him to prevent the lynching. But he finds he's pitched himself into a bitter feud. Now he is faced with a powerful rancher as his enemy, a crooked marshal, a bevy of hard cases and a gunfighter . . . A veteran of many tight spots, Brady might be making his final stand.

GOLD OF THE BAR 10

Boyd Cassidy

Gene Adams and his riders of the Bar 10 had brought in a herd of steers and been paid. Deciding to visit friends, Adams, Tomahawk, Johnny Puma and Red Hawke retrace an old trail on their way back to Texas. But an outlaw gang trails them, interested in the gold in Adams' saddlebags. And ahead of them two killers have kidnapped Johnny's sweetheart, Nancy . . . Can these legendary riders survive the dangers looming on all sides?

DAKOTA GUNS

Mike Stall

Jack Thorn had become a hunter after some of Quantrill's Raiders, under Captain Charlie Chiles, had killed his wife and child. Now, with only Chiles left, Thorn was trailing him towards the Dakotas. Here the Sioux were squaring up to Custer, and Thorn's old commander, General Hipman, was defending Fort Burr. But Chiles had a new line selling guns to the Sioux . . . If only Jack could track Chiles down, he would prevent the greatest disaster the West might ever know.

REDMAN RANGE

David Bingley

When he rode towards New Mexico territory, Rusty Redman expected to find the Redmans of Redman City friendly to a man with the same surname. His outlook changed, however, when he found Laura Burke fleeing from her Redman kin, fearing for her life, and witnessed Redman hirelings bullying farmers. In Big Bend, he took up arms against their gunslingers and played a highly dangerous part in bringing law and order back to the ordinary people.

BROKEN NOOSE

Luther Chance

John Quarry was just another drifter riding into the town of Faithfull. But to Sheriff Horan and Judge Bream, he was the man who would hang for the murder of the McCrindle family . . . But Doc Sims and the bar girl, Cassie, chose to stand for the stranger's defence. Only then did Quarry reveal his hand, his quest and the dreadful retribution he would wreak on a town lost in the making of its own hell.